across from
indian shore

across from
indian shore

BY BARBARA ROBINSON

ILLUSTRATED BY EVALINE NESS

LOTHROP, LEE AND SHEPARD CO., INC. • NEW YORK

For my father-in-law, John F. Robinson,
who lived across from Indian Shore

across from
indian shore

chapter 1

Luke Mitchell didn't rightly know what he was going to tell his mother, or what he was going to tell his brother John. "Although," as he said to himself, scrunching through the pine needles back to the path, "most likely I won't have to tell them, for they'll know just as soon as I get upwind of the cottage."

He was good and ashamed of himself, after all his promises, to go and get mixed up with another skunk. But on the other hand, it was downright contrary of the skunks to look so friendly and peaceable and then

9

turn on a fellow so fast. Luke had caught nearly every kind of animal there was in the woods around the lake and tamed one or two of them, and he wanted a skunk in the worst way, but he just couldn't seem to get the knack of catching them.

John said there wasn't any knack to it, and the best plan was to leave the skunks to go their way, and Luke go his, and not bother one another. Luke had promised to do that very thing, and yet here he was!

Maybe, he thought, if John had already gone into Middleboro with the garden stuff for market, and if his mother was somewhere around the other side of the cottage, he might be able to sneak in without any-one seeing him. He stopped behind the barn to listen and look: the rackety old car was gone, so that meant John had left, and he didn't hear his mother singing, so that meant she was at least out of earshot.

But he forgot about Massie. He had sneaked off that morning early without the dog, because Massie was even a worse hand at catching skunks than Luke himself. But now the dog saw him and came bound-ing off the back porch, ears flapping up and down, and barking welcome. Then all of a sudden he stopped, put his nose up in the air, howled and went kiting back to the house, his tail tucked between his legs and making enough racket for ten dogs.

Mrs. Mitchell opened an upstairs window. "Who's there?" she called. Then she saw Luke and, what was worse, smelled him. "Oh, Lucas! Not again! Well, get the shovel and bury your clothes out back of the barn before you come another step!"

He guessed he must have the biggest part of his clothes buried out here, but there wasn't anything else to do. One good thing, John wasn't around. But he heard all about it at supper that night.

"What you want, Luke," he said, "is something to keep you busy. You're too big a boy to waste your time this way . . . especially now."

Especially now meant now that Pa was not with them, now that they were going to live in the summer cottage all year round, now that John was the man of the family.

"First off," John said, "we've got to make the garden bigger, for I can sell in town twice what we grow. Then we've got to lay back food for the winter too. And when you feel like you've got to have a ramble through the woods, why, do it to some purpose. You can take a pail along and pick blueberries. I can sell the berries by the pint, and I can sell Mother's blueberry pies. Then we've got to widen the path out to the road and keep it cut back. Then we've got to dig out a root cellar. Then we've got to keep chopping wood and piling it up in the pump room against the cold weather, for it's all we'll have for heat this winter. So you see, Luke, you'll hardly have much time for skunk-trapping. Or many more clothes to spare!" He chuckled and then leaned over and slapped Luke on the back. "We've cut out a big job for ourselves, moving out here to the lake to live . . . no use to pretend it isn't."

Luke was silent. It might be a big job, but to his way of thinking, you could travel all the places there were in the world and never find a better place to live than here in the cottage, on the shore of Lake Onagawan. For as long as he could remember they had spent their summers here at the cottage, and the worst day of every year was always that day in September when they went out the path to the road for the last time. Luke would turn around backwards in the seat so he could see the last of everything till the next year. Now that would never happen again: they had sold the house in Middleboro, and the cottage was home forever and always, all year long.

Pa had built the cottage when he was a very young man, but then it was just a cabin in the woods. He added the big kitchen when he married, and extra rooms as the family grew—a porch here, a shed there, just as he felt like it. There were no other cottages

around, for most people didn't like being way out in the middle of the forest. The nearest town was Middleboro, twelve miles away, and Pa had cut a path out to the main road, wide enough for the old car to get through.

There were any number of foot-broken paths here and there through the woods—every one familiar to Luke—and secret places Pa knew about, back deep in the forest where the trees grew so thick it was always dusk-dark.

One path led to the Sentinel Pine—an old giant of a pine tree that stood up far above all the other trees in the forest, bare of branches except at its tiptop.

"Wouldn't it be grand," Pa would say, "if we could somehow contrive to climb it? What couldn't we see?" But not even the squirrels ever tried to climb the Sentinel Pine.

There was a path, too, to Iron Brook—the thin thread of brick-red water that seemed to spring right out of the rocks around it and tasted of nails; there were paths to the best blueberry bushes and paths shared with deer; there was a path to the Judgment Rock, a high flat outcropping of stone, set down right in the middle of the forest—the Indians' council rock, Pa said.

There were shallow caves—just big enough for

Luke and Massie to get in out of a sudden shower and sit on a carpet of pine needles, perfectly dry, while curtains of rain fell all around them. There were deep black caves with cold clammy walls where water dripped constantly. There were nighttime places, like Bullfrog Swamp and Owl Hollow . . . nothing remarkable by day, but at sundown the frogs tuned up their bass drum throats and the owls went hoo-hooing through the pines—a perfect orchestra, they were. There was Red Eagle River, flowing around and through the forest, and Quitticum Pass where, in dry weather, you could walk right along in the river bed.

And there was Minitik Island, a distant fuzzy line of trees that Pa pointed out as they stood on the lake shore. It was midway across the lake—heavily wooded, or so Pa guessed, though no one really knew. No one ever went to Minitik Island; no one fished close to its shore. It was a haunted island, and though there were many stories about it, no one knew which were true and which were not. Some said it was an island made all of fog. Some said it was a floating island, or that it was all quicksand and marsh; that the wind on Minitik had a human voice, that there was no wind there at all, ever; that it was haunted by evil spirits, that it was haunted by good spirits . . . no one dared to find out.

And last of all, best of all, most important of all the things or places Pa knew . . . there was, across the lake from the cottage, Indian Shore and the Princess!

John was still talking, Luke suddenly realized, and talking to him. "It'll be hard for you, Luke, but you must understand that this summer will be different from the others. You mustn't think of it·as a vacation."

"One thing you forgot," Luke said. "We've got to get the boat out and tighten her up. That was the very first thing Pa did every summer; tighten up the boat and get her down to the water."

John cleared his throat and pushed his chair back from the table. "We've got no time to fool with the boat. We can't use the boat for anything, you see. But we need the garden, and the root cellar and the wood."

His mother put her hand on Luke's arm. "Maybe," she said, "there'll be a day when we can spare the time for the boat. We'll see." She nodded across the table at John.

"Well, I guess you're right," he said. "I'll tell you . . . tomorrow morning while I'm in town you chip off the old paint the best you can and I'll help you in the afternoon. We'll get her caulked, and then you can paint her yourself." He raised a warning finger. "But I don't want to find you down rowing around the rushes all hours. After your chores are done you can fool in the boat, but not before."

John sounded stern, but Luke knew he didn't mean to be. It was just that John now had so much responsibility.

"And then, John," Luke went on, "some day you'll row me over across the lake, won't you?"

"Row you across the lake! What for?"

Luke couldn't believe his ears. Surely his brother had not forgotten!

"We can't go joy riding this summer." John took his plate to the sink and then went out the back door, whistling for Massie.

"What is it, Luke?" his mother asked.

"Why, the Princess!" he said. "The Princess and the tribe . . . I'm almost eleven years old now, and Pa said . . ."

She sighed. "Oh, yes. I'd forgotten."

His mother, too! What was wrong with everybody that they could forget the most important thing in the world to him? Here he had waited all his life, or all his life that he could remember, to be ten-going-on-eleven, to row across the lake, to meet the Princess Weetonawammet, maybe to sit in the council around the campfire.

"Not until you're . . . oh, ten-going-on-eleven," Pa

had said. "The Indians say that is when a boy begins to be a man, and can take his place in the life of the tribe. Before that he is a child. You don't want me to take a child to the council fire, do you? The Princess wouldn't take any notice of you. She would send you to play with the children, and you wouldn't like that. No, we'll wait for your tenth summer."

Luke didn't beg or plead to go before then. After all, Pa knew best. Pa and the Princess were friends, and at least once every summer Pa rowed the long way across the lake to the camp and left Luke sitting in the sand at the shore, trying to imagine how it was at the council fire.

When he was very little and hadn't any better sense, Luke had a picture in his mind of many braves in war paint, of tomahawks and talking drums. Many a man would have let him believe this picture, exciting and shivery as it was, but Pa always told the truth and the way he told it, it was even better.

"There are no braves any more," Pa said. "Don't you see, Luke, the Princess is the last of her tribe—once part of the Wampanoag nation. The Wampanoags were here before ever a white man came. They saw the Pilgrims land on Plymouth Rock."

Luke had been to Plymouth and he could picture all that Pa said.

"Then there was nothing here but forest: no Plymouth town, no houses or streets, no Middleboro . . . just miles and miles of forest, and Wampanoag Indians watching from behind the trees while that little boat sailed into the harbor. Think how that must have been!" Pa's eyes always lighted up when he told about it. "I can never make up my mind which was braver—those people coming all the way across the ocean to a country they didn't know anything about; or the Indians, without knowing who this other crowd was or what they were up to, electing to make friends of them instead of tomahawk targets. I like to think it was Massasoit who decided to take that chance." Massasoit was Pa's great favorite, so Luke knew all about him: that he was the Sachem of the Wampanoags, the big Chief. Luke had seen a statue of Massasoit, on a hill in Plymouth, turned bronzy-green from the salt sea spray, and when you looked at that statue you just knew that any man that big and powerful-looking was bound to be the head of it all.

"Now the Princess," Pa went on, "is Massasoit's great-great-great-great-great-great-granddaughter. That's a lot of greats, but you see what it means. She's the last of her family, the last of a wonderful tribe."

"She must be old," Luke said.

"Old, yes, and proud and wonderful to see and

19

know and have for a friend. No, there are no more braves, but when you talk to the Princess and sit at her fire, you can almost feel them all around you, in the trees. You can almost hear them running, and the swish of their arrows. But you'll see. You'll see, when you are ten years old."

And now he was past ten years old, this summer, but Pa was gone. And John didn't put much stock in the Princess, and his mother had forgotten. Luke didn't know whether it was fitting that he should go across the lake alone; there was ceremony to be followed in meeting an Indian Princess. You couldn't just mosey along and say, "Here I am." That was a child's way, and she wouldn't take any notice of him.

Besides, the simple fact was that he couldn't row the heavy boat across the lake. It was too far, the widest lake in the state. He could pole himself along the shore and he could row out to the rushes—clumps of water-rooted reeds growing some twenty-five or thirty feet away from shore—but even that worried his mother, because of the storms. There were lake squalls that blew up in such a hurry you couldn't even see them come, and then the water boiled up and tossed and pitched worse, John said, than the ocean, and a boy in a rowboat wouldn't stand any show at all against that. It was terrible to be on this shore, and the Princess on the opposite shore and no way to get across.

His mother came looking for him the morning after the boat was painted and found him standing at the shore, looking first at the boat, then at all that wide water, and then the other shore so far away and indistinct.

"Luke," she said, "it doesn't help just to stand and look. And there's digging to do in the garden. John can't do it all, and he depends on you."

"If I could only just *see* her!" Luke said. "Pa probably told her. She might just be looking for me to come."

"I know." His mother put her arm around him. "But, maybe, if you do all your chores and help John all you can, and don't pester him about the Princess, he might change his mind. That could be a reward."

The more Luke thought about that, the better it sounded. So he got the spade and the pitchfork from the barn and, with Massie trotting beside him, went out along the path to the garden patch. They had never had a very big garden—just enough for summer vegetables and some over that his mother canned. They had never bothered with potatoes or squash or any winter-keeping vegetables, but John put in a whole plot of potatoes this year, and he scattered

21

squash seeds all around the edges of the garden. Already the squash had sprouted and some vines were spreading out. And John had staked up the tomato plants, and the rows of carrots were all feathery and green. That was just like John; some ways he was more grown-up, even, than Pa.

"First things first," John had said, and he meant staking tomato plants long before they would need to be staked.

"First things first," Pa had said, but he meant tramping through the woods, breaking a new path, trailing a raccoon.

To Luke, there was just one first thing: to meet the Princess Weetonawammet. But he would have to go the long way around about it; he would have to go John's way—work as hard as he could and do every chore that was put to him, and let the skunks alone and generally behave himself, so that John would have to give in and take him across to Indian Shore.

chapter 2

Many times in the next week Luke looked at John's garden and wondered how in the world he ever got it spaded up and planted. It seemed to him that the only crop fit to grow here was rocks; he couldn't stick his pitchfork in the earth without fetching up a rock, big ones and little ones. Some days he would spend as much as an hour just wrestling one big boulder out of the way.

But as the days went along he began to take satisfaction in the big pile of rocks he had dug out. The prettiest ones he set aside to be washed and polished

up and used someday for paperweights or his mother's rock garden or just for a collection of his own. He pretended to himself that he wasn't digging a garden at all, but really collecting rocks, and that made the whole thing a lot more fun.

There were other ways, too, to make work seem less like work and more like something you'd pick to do. Some days Luke would pack a lunch, and a bone for Massie, and at noontime they would go off into the woods till they found a spot where the sunlight filtered through the treetops. Then they would lie on the warm pine needles, still as could be, and watch the little animals—the rabbits and squirrels and, sometimes, a raccoon—scurry around in the underbrush and then, very slowly, peer out from behind bushes and come a little closer and a little closer.

Massie wasn't much of a hand at this game, though. Luke would keep his arm around the dog to keep him quiet, but as soon as a furry nose poked out to sniff the air, Massie would start to quiver and when he couldn't stand it any more, off he would bound . . . to make friends. But of course the rabbit or the coon, or whatever it happened to be, couldn't know that Massie was friendly and they'd be gone just that fast.

But it was the nicest kind of way to have lunch, and if some pine needles or things got mixed up in the sandwiches it didn't really matter. One day they saw a big fat skunk waddling along just as open as could be, as if he knew there wasn't anyone fool enough to take out after him, and he was right. Luke didn't even make a try at catching him, though his fingers itched to. But the one thing he didn't need now was to come home one more time smelling of skunk. That would finish him with John, and John was his only hope of getting across to Indian Shore.

He didn't dare mention it yet, for John never seemed to have a minute to spare. He was up almost before daylight and off to town with a load of vegetables and before you could turn around here he'd be back again, digging in the root cellar. Or if he wasn't doing that, he was clambering around on the roof tightening shingles and fixing leaks that would make it mighty cold in the winter weather. Or he was hoeing in the garden, or he was cutting firewood; he was the busiest human alive.

Once Luke tried to trick him into going across the lake. They were sowing seed in the newly dug garden and when they got to the corn, Luke put up his hoe. "Guess we better hold off now till we get the fish, hadn't we?"

"What fish?" John asked.

"Well, we're going to plant a fish along with the corn, aren't we? That's the best way, isn't it?"

"Where'd you get such a notion as that?"

"Why, from Pa. He said that was the way the Indians . . ." He stopped short and bit his lip. He hadn't intended to say anything about Indians.

John grinned. "Indians, again, huh? Well, Pa was right. So they did put a dead fish in with the corn, for fertilizer. But nowadays we spade the fertilizer right into the ground, so we don't need to bother with the fish." He went right on measuring off his furrows, and Luke saw now that it wasn't any use. But it was a good plan, anyway. They wouldn't catch any fish in close to shore, he knew; they would have to row nearly to the middle of the lake and he thought, once there, he could talk John into going the rest of the way.

"You don't think the fish would be better?" he asked.

"No, I don't." John raised an eyebrow. "You didn't have any ideas about maybe doing our fishing on the other side of the lake, now did you?"

Luke's face reddened—how did John know that?

Still, he didn't get mad, or say no; he even smiled a little. So, maybe, if they ever got all this everlasting work done, there would come a day when he would say, "Yes, we'll go across the lake today." And then Luke would get ready. He had it all planned. He would take a bath, even if it should happen to be in the middle of the day, and put on his best shirt and soak his head so his hair would lie down flat.

The thing he couldn't decide was what to take for a present. Pa always took a present when he went to visit the Princess—a pie, or a loaf of fresh bread. Once he took a whole half-turkey that was meant for a meal, and Mother only smiled and said, "Well, Adam, if you must, you must."

Luke thought these were queer gifts. "Shouldn't you take some beads or truck like that?" he had asked, but Pa said the Princess Weetonawammet was too practical a woman to look for beads if there were turkeys available.

But there hadn't been any turkeys around the cottage for a long, long time and Luke didn't quite see how he could make off with a whole pie or a pan of biscuits, and not have somebody notice the loss. There wasn't so much food but that any disappearances had to be accounted for.

It was Massie who finally showed him the very thing to take.

They had been gathering wild blackberries all day —a job Luke hated, for the bushes were prickly and the berries were small and you had to watch all the time for snakes, but his mother made a wild blackberry jam which almost made the tedious job worth while. Massie had stayed close by him for a while and then bounded off on business of his own, back from the path into the deep woods, where the trees grew thick enough to shut out light and the underbrush piled up shin-high in places.

It was nearly sundown, time to head for home, but though Luke whistled and called and whistled again, there was no answering bark and Massie didn't come. It wasn't like him; no matter how far afield he roamed, the dog always came running when he was called.

He must have wandered very deep into the forest and Luke hesitated to go after him. The sun went down fast and darkness closed in quickly in the thick of the woods where there was never much light, even at high noon. But Massie might have fallen in an animal hole or hurt himself some way, so Luke set down his pails and started off to the left of the path, calling as he went. He kept close watch of where he was and didn't turn to left or right, so he could find his way back out again, and he marked his way with a big tree here, or a lightning-blasted tree there. If he had a knife he could blaze marks as he went, as the Indians had done, but lacking a knife he had to use his eyes and his memory.

He had never been so deep in the forest before, even with Pa, and now he began to worry about getting out again. He hadn't called for quite a while—off here in the middle of nowhere with dark night all around, he wasn't too sure what might answer him.

Then, far up ahead, he heard Massie barking—a series of short barks, not hurt, but playful. He followed the sound and found the dog crouched before a thicket of low brambles.

"What's the matter with you?" Luke said. "Making me come all this way. Come on, boy."

But Massie only yipped again, softly, for all the

world like a person saying, "Not so loud. Not so loud, or we'll frighten them away," and he inched closer to the thicket.

It was then Luke saw the eyes, peering out from the brambles . . . two bright spots in the darkness.

It was a baby fox, a red fox, more scared by a considerable sight than Luke himself.

"A fox!" he breathed. He had only ever seen a fox as a quick blur through the trees—they were so fast, and so clever. He could never hope to catch one, but this was only a baby, huddled close to the ground.

He tied Massie to the nearest tree with a length of ropy vine and then, ever so slowly, moved closer, talking softly to the fox. He wished he hadn't left his berries back by the road, but he did have the crusts of his lunch sandwich and he held those out to the animal.

"Come on out," he coaxed, in the same low tone of voice. "Come on out. We won't hurt you. Come on out. How did you get away from all your kin? Massie's tied to a tree and, anyway, he only wants to make friends. Come on out. Here's a crust for you."

The fox moved the tiniest step forward, but Massie growled deep in his throat and the fox froze.

"You hush!" Luke told the dog, "or I'll fetch you a good one!"

31

Massie, looking mournful, lay down at the base of the tree like a naughty child.

Through the stillness Luke could hear the night sounds: the snap of branches as animals crept out to see what was what, the rustle of leaves where an old grandfather hoot owl got himself situated for the night on a tree limb. But Luke didn't hurry. He knew you couldn't hurry with a wild animal, but had to go slowly and never make a sudden sound or a sudden move. Even when the fox crept out and took the crust of bread, Luke didn't offer to lay a hand on him, but only crouched close, talking softly.

It was a very young fox, little more than a ball of chestnut-red fur with two pointed ears and a white-tipped tail, but it was old enough to be cautious and kept its head cocked, watching Luke, as if trying to decide what kind of thing he was.

Massie, bored with the whole business, and with his nose a little out of joint because he was tied to a tree, grumbled, and Luke expected the fox to dash back to cover. But instead, the fox trotted over to Massie and sniffed around him and then rolled over on the ground, all four black paws up in the air. He wriggled around, cuffing Massie's ears and nipping at him, and then suddenly ran off a few feet, planted himself firmly and put his little head back and barked—the loud clear

sharp bark of a fox that carries so far through the still forest.

Massie looked so surprised Luke had to laugh. The dog raised his head, ears flapping up, and if dogs had eyebrows Massie would have cocked his at this noisy red mite of an animal.

The fox barked again and danced off a few steps. "Come on and play, you lazy thing," he was saying.

Luke untied Massie and warned him at the same time. "You be gentle," he said, "gentle."

Then he sat back and watched them make friends. First the fox nipped at Massie and ran all around him furiously, yipping; then he flopped over on his back, waving his paws in the air.

Massie didn't seem to know what to do about it. He just let himself be nipped at for a while, and then when things got too noisy he planted one paw in the fox's middle and looked over at Luke.

"What have we got here?" he seemed to say.

When they started back to the path the fox was perfectly content to come along, nipping at Massie's heels and then dashing off into the trees and back again, playing just like any kind of baby thing. Luke was so busy watching the two of them he almost missed the trail markers; it was hard enough spotting the landmarks as it was.

When the woods thinned out he could see the moon over the path to the cottage. He was surely going to catch it good and proper when he got home. It was long past suppertime and on top of that, something had turned his berry pails over and all the berries were spilled out on the ground.

"That might have been some of your folks," he told the fox, but he had about made up his mind that the fox was an orphan or it wouldn't have been off that way all by itself.

Back of the barn Luke stopped to think over the situation. He was sure there would be a good bit said about his being so late, and he didn't know whether this was the best time to produce a wild animal—baby or not—in his mother's kitchen.

"You keep an eye on the fox," he told Massie, who slept outdoors under the porch. From the looks of things, Massie would have a pretty lively night.

His mother was waiting on the porch, and off down the road he could see John walking up from the lake.

"Here he is!" his mother called. "He's here, John."

She hugged Luke and then she shook him good, as if she couldn't make up her mind which to do. "Where in the nation have you been? Son, it's ten o'clock at night. Your brother's been all around and down to the lake and I don't know where all! We thought you'd . . .

well, we didn't know!" And then she shook him again. And then she hugged him again. "Now tell me what you've been doing all this . . . no, wait till you've had your supper. I'll warm it up."

John wasn't so easy to put off. He wanted to know, right away, just what Luke was doing in the woods until ten at night, and when he heard he shook his head.

"Trapping a fox!" he exclaimed. "What in the world do you want with a fox? And where is it?"

"Out back with Massie," Luke said. "It's just a baby."

"Well, you don't think it's going to stay out back with Massie, do you? You can't bring a wild animal in out of the woods and expect it just to settle down like a lap dog."

But when John went out and looked, there was the fox curled up by Massie in the back yard, playing with Massie's tail.

"Well," John said, "I don't know. I don't know whether it'll be there come morning. And I don't know what you want to do with it."

Luke had his mouth full of supper and didn't have to answer; he was glad of that because he knew exactly what he was going to do with the fox. He had known when he looked back on the path and saw the animal stepping daintily along, its red coat gleaming in the moonlight, its brushy tail held high and proud. He was going to give the fox to the Princess for a present.

And for the first time he was glad John had not taken him across the lake before, because he didn't want to take a playful ball of fur for a present; he wanted to take a grown fox, with his keen hunter's eye and sense of smell and his full plume of waving, white-tipped tail.

Luke lay in bed that night, too excited to think, and tried to decide what to name his fox. He went over in his mind all the Indian words and names Pa used to tell him, but most of them were hard to say—cere-monial names, not very useful for everyday.

While he studied about it he heard again under his window that sharp clear bark, echoing back into the pines.

Wasn't the best name after all just Tokalaluta—Red Fox?

"Tokala," he said aloud several times, rolling the sound around on his tongue. "Tokala." And then, sat-isfied, he plumped up the big down pillow, buried his head in it and fell sound asleep.

CHAPTER 3

The next morning Luke was up, and down the back stairs before the sun was clear up, even before John was awake. He took a few heels of bread from the kitchen and went out back, but there was no fox there.

Massie, of course, came bounding out from under the porch, all wag and wiggle, but he didn't get much of a welcome. Luke was too disappointed.

"Fine watcher you are!" he grumbled at the dog, and Massie slunk back under the porch, ashamed of himself without quite knowing why.

The birds were just waking up: there was a nest of

blue jays under the eaves of the barn and from all the rustling and twittering it sounded for all the world like a houseful of kids all trying to get into the bathroom at once, and having pillow fights, and generally stirring up the house. Luke could hear the mother bird chirping too—a businesslike sound, and a little quarrelsome. "You kids quit this foolishness," she was saying, Luke guessed. And then off she flew—a brilliant streak of blue in the first rays of the sun—up into the treetops, glad, probably, to get out of the house for a while. And then back down to earth to go about her business and get some breakfast for everybody.

He was so busy watching the blue jay, and listening to the squawky commotion in the nest, that he didn't see where the fox came from. Suddenly he was just there, in the middle of the path, pointed ears quivering and one paw held up in the air as if he stopped in midstep.

"Tokala!" Luke called, and Tokala trotted over to him, to nuzzle in his hand and take a piece of bread.

Luke wasn't so silly as to believe the fox knew his name first off, but he would in time. In time too, he thought, grinning, Massie would get used to this fuzzy new friend. Right now the dog was trying his best to scrunch down under the porch and get an extra forty winks of sleep. But Tokala would have none of that.

He crawled right under the porch, too, and yipped and nipped and worried poor Massie out into the sunshine to play.

Massie yawned and shook himself and looked sorrowfully at Luke and then, after one particularly hard nip, swatted Tokala a good blow.

"I said you be gentle!" Luke warned, but Tokala didn't seem to mind at all. He came prancing back for more.

Luke wondered where he had gone in the night: back into the woods, maybe, looking for his family. Tokala was still pretty young to fend for himself in the forest. He wouldn't know yet what to look out for or how to take care of himself, and Luke decided to build a pen for him behind the barn.

There were all kinds of odds and ends of lumber lying around the cottage and John had bought a big coil of chicken wire to fence off the garden from rabbits. He should be able to make a pretty good pen, big enough so the fox wouldn't feel caged.

"Well, look at this!" John was standing on the porch, and he reached down and picked up the fox: "Look at this fellow. I sure didn't think he'd be here this morning."

"He went off during the night," Luke said, "but he came back. Seems to me he's pretty little to take care of himself yet, so I thought I'd build him a pen back of the barn. Maybe there'd be some wire left over from doing the garden fence."

"We'll see, we'll see." John put his arm around Luke's shoulders. "But you don't want to get too attached to him. You know, a fox is a fox. All his instincts are to run wild, and no matter how much he comes to love you, there'll come a day . . . or, more likely, a night . . . when those instincts will be stronger than anything else, and he'll be gone."

Luke crossed his fingers behind his back. He intended to see to it that that didn't happen.

"Now come on in and have your breakfast," John said. "Lots of work to do today."

If Luke thought his chores would ease up, now that the garden was in, he was surely mistaken. John could think up more things for a body to do than there were hours in the day. There was always the root cellar, and the house repairs, and wood to chop. And now John had in mind to grow Christmas trees. Luke was all in favor of that idea, because he didn't see that there would be any work to growing Christmas trees in the middle of a Christmas tree forest, but if there was some way to make work of it, John could find that way all right.

There had been a fire in a section of the woods out to the left of the cottage two years before, and the blackened skeletons of trees still stood, dead barren, but all

41

around and under them were new trees sprouting up. Now John said they must clear out all the dead wood and let the new growth have space to bush up, and light to grow tall. He wouldn't let Luke do the chopping down. John did that himself with Pa's big axe, but then it was Luke's job to haul off the wood, and a mortal hard job it was, too.

Some nights he would be so tired he fell asleep over his supper and many a day he dozed over his lunch sandwich, out in the quiet forest. And then he would dream, or remember—he was never sure which—about the days when Pa would take him along on a tramp; all along the shore, for instance, on a day when a storm was brewing and the sky was gray overhead and the lake restless. Or down the opposite way past White Banks, or, best of all, right up to the top of White Banks —the mountain of sand piled up by onshore winds. From the top of White Banks you could see across the lake to Indian Shore, where the Princess was, waiting for Luke to be ten years old, going-on-eleven.

As the days went by, Luke grew impatient. The summer was slipping by, slipping by, and he was no closer to meeting the Princess than he had ever been. And there didn't seem to be any chance that John would offer to take him. Each time they finished one big job, another one came along. The day they had finally cleared the Christmas tree grove so that nothing was left but even rows of young spruce trees, Luke was all ready to ask, but that was the very day John found extra work to do in town—only two or three hours a day, but that was three hours more he wouldn't be able to row across the lake.

And with every day that passed, Tokala grew—in size and, as Luke could see, in woodsy wisdom. He was faster than Massie, smarter, and better at hiding. Many a time while they played around Luke as he worked, he would see Tokala suddenly stop, ears up and nose in the air, frozen still at some sound or scent, while Massie went on chasing his tail in a circle or whatever other game occupied him. It might be a pheasant, or a rabbit. Luke could never see it, but Tokala always knew and he would slink to the ground and then dart off, that fast, into the brush.

He was never able to catch his game, though, for Massie would look around, find his friend gone, and tear off after him into the brambles, barking and waving his tail around and snapping twigs and branches and throwing leaves up in the air. It was a good thing, Luke thought, that Massie didn't have to catch his food or he'd starve to death.

Luke had only to call and they would come back to him: Massie dashing in and out between the trees, barking furiously at squirrels and chipmunks, but Tokala came silently—a flame of fur darting unseen through the low brush. Luke thought it was a shame; now that Massie was used to having someone to play with, Tokala had outgrown playfulness. He seemed to sense that his proper job was hunting, and his proper place the forest. Luke wondered if John could be right about wild things and their instinct.

He had finished the fox pen, by working after supper as long as the light held or till his mother called him in. It was a funny-looking contraption, he knew, made out of every kind of stray thing he could find. The back wall of it was solid—old planks from the barn that he nailed together—and two sides were chicken wire he begged from John. The other side had him stumped for a long time; he wanted something open, and yet solid, but there wasn't any more wire and not much prospect of getting any.

Then one day John came home from Middleboro with an old bed spring tied to the top of the car. He had found it lying on top of the Middleboro dump.

"I thought you might have some use for it," he said to his mother.

"It may be better than the one that's on Luke's bed," she said. "You try it and see. Too bad to throw away something that still has good in it."

But the minute Luke saw it he knew it would be the very thing to finish the fox pen; and after everyone

had slept on it once and complained of sore bones all
the next day, his mother gave it to him. So that was the
other side of the pen, or part of the other side.

The spring alone wasn't long enough, because Luke
had made the pen to stretch well back into the brush
behind the barn so he made a swinging gate from the
bark of some slim trees. He even left clumps of berry-
bushes inside the enclosure, thinking Tokala might not
even realize he was penned up.

And he seemed not to, for a while.

Then one night Luke sat bolt upright in bed, wakened suddenly for no reason that he could think of, unless it was the full moon making a path as bright as day in his bedroom window.

Then, far off in the forest behind the cottage, he heard the bark of a fox, ringing clear through the still night air. And he heard Tokala answer.

Massie, who had been a little too gay around a bramble bush that day and was suffering a thorn-stuck paw and hurt feelings, was sleeping at the foot of Luke's bed, and now he stirred awake and yipped too.

The fox barked again, but there was no sound from Tokala this time.

"You stay here," Luke whispered to the dog. He had a funny feeling that something was not quite right.

As he crept downstairs and out the kitchen door, Luke was amazed to see how bright everything was in the moonlight. The old kitchen clock said 2:30; he had never been up and around at any such time before and he thought how different everything seemed in the middle of the night.

When he stepped off the porch he could hear hoptoads scattering in all directions, and he walked slowly and cautiously so as not to step on any that didn't get out of the way fast enough.

Then he saw the gate to the pen swinging back and forth, its catch loose. Tokala was gone.

Gone for the night, he wondered? Or gone for good? Suppose Tokala found that other fox, and found a place to live in the woods, and remembered—as John said he would—how it was to be a wild thing?

There was a game Pa used to play when he was trying to figure something out. If he couldn't find his pipe, for instance, he would say, "Now if I were a pipe, where would I be?" And sure enough, nine times out of ten, he'd find the pipe wherever he thought would be a good place. Or if he'd borrowed a pie from the pantry, and that pie was supposed to be part of supper, he'd say, "Now if I were your mother, what kind of story would I believe about what happened to that pie?" That was a joke, of course, because Mother always knew what had become of any missing pies. But it was a good game, all the same, and made you see all sides of a question.

So now Luke asked himself, "If I were Tokala and I found that other fox—one of my own kind—would I come back here to be penned up?" And he knew he wouldn't.

But Tokala wasn't just any fox. He was a present for the Princess, and Luke started off down the path to bring him back.

This was the second time Luke had ever been back in the forest after dark. It was easier this time because of the full moon—bright even through the dense trees.

47

Any time of night was about like any other in the woods, but he *knew* it was 2:30 in the morning and that made a difference. Pa always said that after midnight the forests belonged to the animals and the owls and all the night creatures, and Luke saw what he meant.

He felt as if there must be a thousand eyes watching him from branches and from under old logs and burrows, wondering what he was doing here where he had no business to be.

He was surprised to find himself at the base of the Council Rock—it just showed how turned around a person could get, how mixed up in directions. He had no idea he had gone that deep into the woods.

He clambered up the jutting rocks to the flat table of stone and looked around. The Council Rock was no Sentinel Pine, of course, or even as tall as a medium-sized tree, but he could see around him farther than if he were standing flat on the ground. There was no sign of Tokala, though, in any direction.

On the far side of Council Rock the stones were broken and split, forming fissures and holes. His foot slipped on one of these and before he could get balanced, his whole body slid, smooth as butter, down between these rocks and landed on the cold mossy bottom under the Rock, on the floor of what appeared to be an underground cave.

Here there was no bright moon to show him where he was—only a single beam of cold light shining down through the hole where he had fallen, and beyond that pool of light there was nothing but blackness. The walls, when he touched them, were clammy and wet to his hand, and he could hear water dripping around him.

The trouble was that, having gotten in, he didn't see any way to get out again. The sides of the split were smooth with no foot or hand holds to help him up. He tried jumping, but he couldn't jump high enough to grasp the outer edges of the hole. There must be another opening somewhere, he knew, but the thought of creeping along those damp walls in the pitch black made him break out in a sweat, chilly as he was. Still, he couldn't just sit there, and as his eyes became more accustomed to the darkness he walked along slowly, feeling his way.

The cave widened out as he went and the bottom seemed to drop away little by little and then, with no warning, it split in two directions, one path leading straight ahead and one off to his left.

"If I was an opening to this cave, where would I be?" he asked himself, but the game didn't work as well on caves as it did on borrowed pies.

Luke wasn't frightened. Oh, he knew there were

such things in the world as bottomless caves, where people fell in and were never seen or heard of again; and he knew there were caves where people got trapped by rockslides and had food sent down to them by hollow pipes, and gasped their last dying words up the same hollow pipes . . . but if there had been any such thing around the cottage he would have heard about it.

This was just a plain ordinary cave—deeper than most, but that was all—and someplace there was an opening to it.

There was, though, one big difference about this cave: it was Luke's. He had found it and it was his own secret place. He meant to come back with a torch and explore it, and he was going to heave another rock over the hole where he slid through so nobody else would ever find it.

It was getting lighter now in the cave and up ahead he could see moonlight, dimly. It was the opening, all right, covered over with brambles and wild growth, and he scrambled out, scratching his hands and arms bloody on the thorns.

It was like magic: from the outside you couldn't tell there was anything there at all. No wonder no one had ever found this place before! It was so much like any other place in the forest that Luke wondered if even he could find it again, but he took careful notice of everything all around. The only thing unusual enough to use for a landmark was a stand of three pines, their bases so close that they seemed to grow almost from the same root. There was that to remember, and he made a rough triangle of stones in front of the cave as an extra sign.

All the way back to the path he made little rock mounds to guide him. He planned to come back with a knife in the daytime and blaze a proper trail, making his signs low on the trees so nobody else would notice them.

In his excitement about the cave, he had almost forgotten what he came out for in the first place, and he could hardly believe his eyes when he rounded the corner by the barn and saw Tokala standing in the middle of the path, waving his brushy tail in welcome.

So, for tonight, the fox was willing to come back to his pen. But how long, Luke wondered, would he be willing? Pretty soon wouldn't there come a night when he would just stay in the forest, when he would forget about Luke and Massie, when they would never see him again except as a flash of red through the trees?

He decided that the time had come to take Tokala to his rightful owner—to the Princess. Tomorrow he would ask John to take him over the lake.

chapter 4

He decided not to say anything about trailing Tokala through the woods. Apparently nobody had waked
up and missed him and as for the scratches, he was
usually pretty scratched up anyway from berrypicking.
He didn't see any cause to worry everybody, now that
it was all over.

He woke up hungry as a bear, and when he stuck
his nose out from under the covers he smelled syrup
bubbling on the back of the stove—clear evidence of a
pancake morning.

Luke had a special way he went at pancakes. First of all he needed three pancakes all at once; four was better, but he could make do with three. Then he made a melting sandwich of pancakes, butter and syrup, spreading each cake with enough butter to make a pool and enough syrup to soak in. Then he poured more syrup over the top, letting it dribble down the sides. Then came the most important part: he counted to ten before he took the first bite. A count of ten was just long enough for all the butter and all the syrup to mingle together so you couldn't tell which was syrup and which was pancake, and what you had was a buttery squish of goodness that tasted better than anything else in the world.

John never would take the time to count to ten, and especially not today. He had a hauling job in Middleboro that would keep him away from home overnight.

"So you'll have to mind things here," he told Luke. "Last thing tonight, be sure the kitchen door is shut tight so no animals can get in. And bury the garbage scraps good and deep; don't just scratch a few pine needles over the top and bring every skunk in the nation right to the door."

John finished his breakfast and went out back, still naming off instructions. "I pulled the boat back from the water, just in case there should be a storm. Doesn't look much like it, but you never can tell. Be sure the kitchen wood box is full so you don't have to go rummaging around when it's suppertime. And be sure the well lid is on tight . . . be pretty if some animal fell in. . . ."

Luke wondered if there would ever be an end to the list, but finally John climbed into the car. "Now you understand, Luke, that you're responsible for the house and for Mother. I'll try to be back by tomorrow night, but if I can pick up another job along the way it might be I'd be gone two nights." He put his hand on the boy's shoulder. "I depend on you."

Luke knew this was a bad time to ask, with John in a hurry and worried about being away, but he just couldn't bear to wait any longer.

"John, now that the garden's all in, and the Christmas tree grove is cleared, and the cellar's more than half dug out, we've done pretty well, haven't we?"

"Pretty well, yes," John said.

"Then, when you get home tomorrow, can we take the day and go across the lake?"

John tightened his lips. "The Indians, again?"

"Please, John."

"Luke, you think the work around here is all finished? Why, we've no more than half begun! You won't think the pump room is so full of wood if there comes a bitter cold day, and snow piled up waist-high, and we'd have to go find something to burn to keep warm. And we've still got all the windows and doors to weather-strip, and we've got to clear another two feet each side of the path here or we'll never get out in the dead of winter."

His words hit like hammers in Luke's ears.

"Now it would take a full day to row over that lake and then back, and we can't spare the time. Besides which—now you won't like this but you'll have to face a thing or two—even if we did go on any such fool trip, what makes you think that old woman is still there? Why, my gracious, she was an old woman when Pa was a boy! It's my belief that she's gone, long ago, and all there is over there is just the other side of the lake. Now you forget it."

And John was gone, clattering off down the narrow path.

Luke stood rooted to the spot. He felt weak in the knees and a little sick to his stomach . . . the Princess couldn't be gone! She couldn't be gone!

He ran down the path to the shore, forgetting his chores and his responsibility, forgetting Tokala, forgetting even Massie, who howled mournfully from the kitchen.

White Banks was blinding white in the early morning sun, and from the top he could look out over the lake to the distant line of trees, far, far over on the other side. And he knew John had to be wrong. But he knew, too, that John would never give in, so what was the use of digging the cellar and setting by things for winter; what was the use of living here all year round if he never met the Princess?

He walked all the way up the shore beyond White Banks, past where Iron Brook emptied into the lake, around the curve of the shore line till he was clear out of sight of the cottage. Then he circled back through the woods, eating berries for lunch, and finally lay down on the floor of the forest under the Sentinel Pine, where he could look straight up through those faraway branches to the blue sky and the pillows of white clouds. All around him was the drowzy hum and click of bugs and the chatter of birds and the warm rich smell of pine, and he dozed off, worn-out from the long walk and, even more, from the terrible fear that now he might never see the Princess, never sit at her campfire, never bring her his present.

When he woke up, the warmth had gone from the pine needles under him and the sun was slanting down toward evening as he came up behind the barn, ashamed to see Tokala, who had been penned up all day. He saw the fresh patch of earth where his mother had buried the garbage scraps, and he was ashamed about that, too.

The cottage was strangely quiet. Usually his mother sang as she worked around the kitchen, but today there was no sound, there or anywhere else in the house. There were pieces of chicken floured and waiting for the skillet, and a pan of biscuits on the sink board, but the fire in the stove was burned down to a fine bed of glowing coals—not a suppertime fire at all. Where was his mother? Where was Massie?

As if in answer he heard Massie bark off to the side of the house, and he followed the sound.

His mother lay, half-propped against the side of the well, and her voice was so weak he could hardly hear it. She had tied her apron string around her leg, above a big, purpling bruise.

"Snake-bite," she whispered. "He was under the well cover when I picked it up. You'll have to run to get me the sharp knife from the kitchen, and whet it on the stone. I didn't know whether I should go for it or not; your pa always said to stay still if you were snake-bit. I called for you," she added, and Luke felt his face flame red with shame.

"Hurry, son," she said.

This was how he took care of his mother while John was away! He could hardly find the knife for the tears in his eyes—tears of anger at himself. He had left her with all his chores to do; it was his job to see to the well cover and of course if he didn't do it, his mother would, and see what had happened! And then he had gone so far he didn't hear her call when she needed him!

He couldn't look when she slashed across the wound with the sharp point of the knife, and then sucked the poison and spit it out. Then he made a sling of his jacket and helped her to the porch.

"Now we've got to have help," she said. "A doctor or someone who will know what to do."

"There's nobody nearer than Middleboro."

"I know, and that's twelve miles. Oh, if only we had a horse, or a bicycle, or something. If only John were here!"

But John wasn't here, and it was Luke's responsibility. "I'll go," he said, "just as fast as I can. I'll run."

"No, don't run, or you'll never get there. Maybe somebody will come along the road."

Massie started to come with him, but Luke sent the dog back. "He'll be company for you," he called, and then started out.

There were three or four different paths out to the main road, but they all wound around and Luke figured he could cut his time by taking a straight line through the woods. But he was too worried to think clearly, and too rushed to get his bearings, and he ended up back behind the barn. He had only gone in a circle, and wasted fifteen minutes.

John said that a good walker could make a mile in fifteen minutes or so. That meant that, even with the best of luck, it would be three and a half hours and maybe more before he even got to Middleboro. Then he would have to find someone, in the middle of the night, and come all the way back again. And all the while his mother must lie out on the porch, alone except for Massie, and hurt.

What would John do? he asked himself . . . but John would just get in the car and drive to Middleboro and that would be that.

What would Pa do? He could almost hear Pa's voice in his ear. "Why, the Princess has forgotten more than you and I could ever hope to learn about living in the woods, about animals, about what berries are poison and what ones aren't; how to tell weather from the moon, how to poultice a bad tooth, or heal any other hurt. . . ."

Pa would get the Princess and she would know what to do.

He slipped around the side of the house and down through the woods to the lake, quietly, so his mother wouldn't hear him, or Massie come running. He didn't

let himself think how far it was to the other side, or whether John might be right, and the Princess gone. He didn't think about the weight of the boat, or the chance of a lake storm. He only thought that he had failed in his responsibility and he had to make it right.

He pulled and tugged the boat into the water and started out. The moon was up full and bright now, making a shiny path out into the middle of the lake. It seemed to Luke that he was seeing more and more things by moonlight lately, and if he hadn't been so worried about his mother and so mad at himself, he might have enjoyed this trip, at least for a while.

But by the end of two hours he didn't feel anything except tired and discouraged. He had about made up his mind that there was no opposite shore at all, that John was right and there was no Princess, there was nothing in the whole world but this everlasting lake of still dark water—trap-water, waiting to suck him in if he leaned too far over. The only sound was the gentle whispering of the ripples against the side of the boat, and a hoot owl somewhere in the distance.

He called to the owl, and he sang aloud, and he talked to the moon—anything so he wouldn't think how far it was still to go, and how heavy the oars were; so, most of all, he wouldn't remember what he had done—gone off all day and left his mother to do for him all he should have done, left the well lid off for a snake to crawl under.

"Ho-oo!" he called to the owl, and the owl hooted back.

"Ho, Mr. Fisherman, I know you mighty well, Got any craw-dads here for to sell?" . . . he sang. It was a song of Pa's and it was a bouncy kind of song, but not out here, echoing back at him from across the water.

Even when, finally, he reached the other side he had no way of knowing how far up or down he might have drifted and he poled himself along the side, brushing through low-hanging trees and shore vegetation until he came to a beaching place and, a few feet ahead, a path back through the trees.

It wasn't much like the path from the lake to the cottage on the other side. This wasn't much more than an animal track and he could see it wasn't much used, for the bushes were growing in on both sides. Now he could hear the rustle of things moving off to the right and left of him: animals, curious and wondering what it was that came to disturb their night.

"Sh-h-h," he said to them. "It's all right. Sh-h-h."

Then suddenly the trees opened and he stood in a cleared place before a ramshackle kind of house. The windows, with no curtains to them, were like eyes looking at him. The porch railing was broken and falling away, so that the house seemed to lean in his direction. And on the rim of the roof sat a hoot owl—the same one, maybe, that had called to him out on the lake. Now, with a harsh beating of its wings, the owl flew past his head and off into the woods, hooting as it went. And then everything was perfectly still, here before the lodge of the Princess.

Now, for a moment, he forgot about his mother and the reason he had come alone across the lake. He had a funny feeling in the pit of his stomach, and a prickling up his spine. It was like waiting all year for the circus to come to town, or waiting on the front porch for the Fourth of July parade to come down Main Street, or waiting for Christmas. The last minute before the show started under the big tent, the last minute before you heard the sound of the parade band, the last minute of the night before Christmas before you ran downstairs—the last minute was always the best of all. This was the last minute of waiting to meet the Princess, and he broke out in goose bumps all over his arms.

Suddenly there was the sharp crack of a shutter and there, in one of the window-eyes where a moment before there had been nothing but blackness, stood the Princess.

She was so old that *old* was not enough of a word. The moonlight, slanting across the window, showed her hair white and she clawed it back from her face with knobby fingers, and her voice, when she spoke, was as crackly as dry twigs on the forest floor.

"Who's that?" she called.

"It's . . . me," Luke said.

"Who's there?"

Again, he could almost hear Pa's voice in his ear, telling him the words to say, the ceremony to use. "I am Lucas Mitchell," he called, "from across the wide water." He even remembered, now, the proper signs to give. "I have come alone to the lodge of the Princess Weetonawammet because my father . . . I have come alone. I ask the help of the Princess for my mother who is sick." It didn't sound right, somehow. "How do you do?" he added.

"Wait there, boy," the Princess said.

"She's snake-bit," he called, "and we don't know what to do."

"Wait there."

The Princess moved as soft as any stalking animal. He didn't even hear a door open, or creak, and there she stood beside him. Close to, her face looked like a crumpled brown-paper grocery bag, or a piece of weathered driftwood, with loose skin and deep hollows, but she wasn't bent and stooped like most old people. She had pulled her hair back to a plait, and she was wrapped in a bright blanket all covered with Indian signs. On her feet were soft moccasins.

"Now," she said, "how did you come here?"

"I rowed."

"Rowed, did you?" She turned and walked away from him down the path to where the boat was beached. There she put her hand to her eyes and looked out over the lake and then, chuckling deep in her throat, she took his arm between her two hands and rolled it back and forth. "Rowed!"

"It's my mother. She's snake-bit, and we cut it, but we don't know what more to do for her."

"Ah-h-h," said the Princess, as if she understood all that. "I have a medicine . . . good for many things, good for snake-bite. I can give you that."

"I thought . . . I thought might be you'd come over with me. I'm all alone there."

"Your father?"

He swallowed hard. "Pa's dead."

66

"Huh," the Princess grunted. She looked down at the boat and across the lake and back to Luke, and then she pulled her blanket around her shoulders. "I won't row," she said.

"I never meant you to row," Luke said, but that was a lie. He had thought of course an Indian . . . a Princess! . . . could row the old boat like a house afire. The very thought of putting his blistered hands to the oars again turned his legs and arms and insides to jelly, but he pushed the boat out and held it steady while the Princess stepped into the bow end and sat down.

The Princess said nothing, and Luke wondered if they were going to row all the way back without a word. If she would just talk, he thought, it might take his mind off the pain in his hands.

"My father would have brought me over to meet you," he said. "I'm ten years old this summer—ten-going-on-eleven. He wouldn't bring me before."

The Princess sighed a long sigh. "Adam Mitchell," she said, pronouncing it Ah-dahm, "was my friend." She began to hum a tuneless sort of song, with words strange to Luke. "Now," she said, when the song was finished, "there is no one left who cares. The bones of my people lie deep under these sands, and I am the last. I sit, lonely, by the waters my people fished, and I am the last. I live, sad, on the lands my people called theirs;

67

the lands ruled by the great Sachem, my many times grandfather. I am the last of his tribe, the last of his blood, and no one cares. Your father, my friend, was the last to care. Boy!"

Luke, lulled by the singsong rhythm of her voice, jumped.

"There was a time when this lake was filled with the canoes of my people, rowing by day to your side for better hunting. There were signal fires lit on your Sand Mountain, so that the tribe was never divided, even by the wide water."

"White Banks," Luke said.

She lapsed into her murmurous chant of sorrow, and Luke, looking to his left, saw in the bright moonlight

their shadow picture: the awkward boat, his own bending form and the straight wrapped figure of the Princess. And, surely, there in front and behind were many slim canoes and feathered figures rowing silently, steadily, slipping through the water, gliding over rushes.

"Boy!" she again commanded his attention. "Then, fish were caught by hand or with arrows. Game . . ." she grunted, as if this were nothing, "game was run to

death. Two swift young men could run a deer to ground. Can you outrun a deer?"

He shook his head.

"Huh." She grunted in satisfaction. "Now, now there is no signal fire on your Sand Mountain. The tribe is never divided. Princess Weetonawammet is the last of the tribe. And no one, no one cares."

"I care," Luke breathed.

"A-h-h." The Princess chuckled again. "Ah-h-h. Lu-kas Mitch-ell, boy-who-rows-by-night. Chasatonga —Little Big Man."

"Chasatonga," Luke repeated. "Chasatonga."

He forgot how sore his hands were and how tired his arms, and almost before he knew it they had reached the other side and he led the Princess up the path to the cottage.

His mother's eyes widened when she saw them.

"I thought she'd know best what to do," Luke said.

"But . . ." his mother looked from one to the other. "How . . . how did . . .?"

"I rowed across," Luke said.

The Princess said nothing beyond an occasional grunt. She looked carefully at his mother's leg and touched, gently, the flesh around the bite and then took from the folds of her blanket a jar of black, sweetish-smelling stuff which she smeared all over the wound.

Then she held out her hands, about a foot apart.

"The snake," she said, "this long?"

"No," said his mother. "Not so big as that."

"Huh. You stay here, quiet," the Princess made a broad gesture, to show the passage of the sun, "all this day. It will heal."

"I thank you," his mother said. "You were good to come at night. Luke should not have bothered you."

"For my friend," the Princess said.

"I'm ashamed not to offer you a hot meal but, Luke," she turned to him, "there's bread and butter and a jar of the blackberry jam, and John brought me some tomatoes this morning from the garden. Find a bite of something for the Princess to eat." She laid her hand on his arm, ". . . and yourself. Then if you care to wait, my son John will be home later and he can take you back across the lake."

The Princess turned slowly and looked at Luke. "This one came for me," she said.

"Well . . ." his mother hesitated. "I just thought . . . it's such a long way and John is a grown man. . . ."

"This one came for me," the Princess said again.

Luke understood what she meant. He had to finish what he started and not leave half the job for John.

"I'll row you back," he said, hoping to goodness that he could, for his arms felt like sticks at his side.

His mother fell asleep then and by the time they had finished a cold snack of bread and jam, dawn was just breaking.

"I've been awake the whole night," Luke said, half to himself, half to the Princess. "Seems like I've spent a lot of my nights up and around lately, like when I fell in the cave and . . ." He stopped, suddenly remembering the best thing of all. "Come out back with me," he said, "there's something here for you to see."

It was something to see, too. Tokala was standing in the center of the fox pen, his full plume of tail held high and his coat glinting red in the first rays of the sun. He came forward, one or two proud steps, and then stopped, cocking his head to watch the Princess.

"There!" Luke said. "When I came to meet you, I was going to bring a present, like Pa did. This is the present. His name's Tokala . . . Tokalaluta."

"Red fox." The Princess nodded.

"I caught him myself, and tamed him. He was only a baby."

"This is for me? Your gift?"

Luke nodded.

The Princess opened the pen gate and stood back. "Go, Tokalaluta," she said.

"But he's yours!" Luke protested. "I tamed him for you!"

The Princess dipped her head very slightly. "I thank you for your gift. The fox will thank me for his freedom."

"He'll come back, I'll bet. I'll bet he won't even go!"

Tokala had stopped in the middle of the path and was looking back toward the barn, toward Luke and the Princess. Then he turned and, with a quick flirt of his tail, stepped daintily into the woods and was gone.

"But he was your present!"

"The catching, the taming, the giving of him, was a present."

Now Massie, who had been asleep under the porch, trotted around the barn to the fox pen. He sniffed all around outside and then went in the gate and sniffed everywhere there. Then he put his head back and howled, but there was no answering bark from the woods.

"Come on, boy," Luke said and the dog, still puzzled, came to his side and pushed his cold nose into Luke's hand.

The Princess watched, for a minute, where Tokala had vanished into the woods and then she turned to Luke. "Are you tired?"

"No," he lied.

"Hold your arm out straight at your side."

He tried, but it fell as limp as a vine.

73

"I will row back," she said, "and you can rest in my lodge."

So he left a note for his mother and told Massie to watch her, and Luke and the Princess walked down the path, still wet with the morning dew. As the Princess rowed them back, she made a song for him. There wasn't much tune to it, and Luke didn't know the words, but he did recognize "Tokalaluta" and "Chasatonga" and he knew it was a song about him.

chapter 5

All in all, John said, it was probably a good thing that everything turned out the way it did. "I won't go on about how you forgot the well cover," he said. "I reckon you were sorry enough about that. And you did the best you could to make it right. And now you've met your Princess, so that won't be eating at you all the time, taking your mind off your work."

But John was wrong. No matter what he was doing, and surely there was enough still to do, Luke couldn't buckle down to work. In the middle of hoeing the garden, or digging in the cellar, something would come over him and he would wander down to White Banks and strain his eyes across the lake. One visit wasn't enough; there were still so many things to ask the Princess. And he had never sat at her council fire and listened to her tell stories by the light of the dancing flames. It seemed like a whole summer wouldn't be long enough to find out all he wanted to know, but there was never any time to spare with all John thought up for him to do.

Now it was to be another garden; more spading and raking and sifting out rocks.

"We'll do it now," John said. "Then next summer that will be one less job. Next summer we've got to work on the house, close in the porch, open another fireplace into the chimney."

Luke sighed. "Won't we ever be through?"

"No," John said, "not for many a long year. What we've got here is a summer cottage, and we've got to make it fit for a year-round house."

So it was back to digging rocks again—even harder now in the full heat of summer. And the harder it got, the lazier Luke got and the more things he forgot to do and the more things he did wrong.

In the hot dry months of midsummer the garden had to be watered every day, and that meant pail after pail

76

of water lugged from the well and poured in the ditches between the rows of plants.

It got so Luke could hardly bear to eat a tomato, considering all the digging it took to get that tomato planted and all the water it took to get that tomato to grow.

"I wonder what people do when they haven't got water," he grumbled one night. It had been the hottest day of all, the air still and heavy, and he had envied Massie who could lie under the porch where it was shady or paddle in the lake to get cool.

"They wish they had it," John said, and his tone was sharp. "We're lucky to have a good deep well. Dry spell like this, lots of wells just dry up."

Luke wished privately that their well would dry up for a day or two; long enough for him to row across the lake and visit the Princess, long enough for him to blaze a good trail to his secret cave, long enough for him to go looking again for Tokala.

Every morning now John studied the sky for signs of rain, but the sun came up broiling hot each day and the pine needles were powdery dust underfoot. John never stood out on the porch with his pipe after supper, he was afraid of stray sparks.

There had been over two weeks of dry heat and one morning Luke decided he couldn't stand it another

minute. He had been wrestling with one big rock, trying to lever it out of the garden with a pole, but he
couldn't budge it. He had promised John to finish his
spading that day, and he had promised to water the
garden before noon, and he had promised to work with
John in the root cellar, but all he could think about was
how cool and dark the inside of his cave was and how
good the damp moss would feel, curling up between
his bare toes.

He leaned once more against the pole with all his
weight—almost hanging on it—and the pole snapped
off clean at the base.

"All right!" he said to no one in particular. "All
right!" It was all the sign he needed, and he laid the
spade and pitchfork down beside the garden and started
back into the woods.

He hadn't gone far when he heard John calling his
name over and over. He stopped, knowing he should
go back. John wouldn't just call for nothing; probably
he came out to the garden and found Luke gone, after
all his promises. Or maybe he'd found some new job
to be done.

I can always say I didn't hear him, Luke thought.
He knew he would get the dickens for leaving his work
this way, but at least he wouldn't get it till tonight
when he got back home.

He found his rock markers all right—scattered, some of them, by animals, which was why rock markers wouldn't do for a permanent trail. The arrow signs he now carved in trees leading back from the path would be better.

John's voice had faded into the distance long before he got to the overgrown entrance to the cave, but most of the joy had gone out of his escape anyway. The dark mossy cavern was just as cool as he thought it would be, but he couldn't take full pleasure in it, knowing that John was out in the full afternoon sun probably digging away at that pesky rock in the garden.

He poked around the cave for a while, halfheartedly, and roamed back through the woods as far as Council Rock, but he couldn't make a good time of it no matter how hard he tried. It was almost a relief to give the whole thing up and start home.

He was well along the path when he first smelled something strange—something out of place—ahead of him in the direction of the cottage. Then he saw the drifts of smoke floating up in the still air and he started to run.

It might be a forest fire, but that would make great billows of smoke and there would be the crackle of burning pine boughs. But if it wasn't a forest fire, then . . . what? He ran harder, and when he turned the

79

curve in the path he saw something missing: the familiar jut of the barn roof with its loose shingles that John said they must fix someday soon.

John himself was standing by the remains of what had been the barn. Now it was a blackened hull of ashes, smelling wet and smoky like a doused campfire.

John's face, too, was black with smoke. "Where were you?" he asked. "I called and called for you to help with the buckets. I was afraid the trees would catch and they would have, too, if there'd been even a breath of wind. Where were you?"

"I . . . I was back in the woods," Luke said, unable to look his brother in the face.

"I see." John sighed. "Well, we needed you. Don't know that we could have saved the barn, but you could have spared Mother and me a little." He kicked at the ashes.

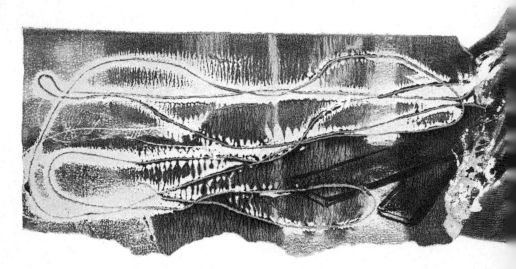

"I'm sorry," Luke said.

"Yes, I reckon you are, but that's not much help now."

"Is the fire all out?"

"Appears to be. I'll stay here though and watch."

"I can do that," Luke said. "I'll sit right here and not move as long as there's any chance it'll start again."

John looked at him for a long, long minute. "Well, Luke, you say you will, but how can I be sure? How can I be sure you won't run off into the woods again?" No," he settled himself on the porch steps, "I'll just sit here and watch."

Luke went into the house slowly. His mother was asleep on the front porch cot; there were smudges of ash on her face, too. He couldn't bear to think of how many buckets of water she must have carried; he knew how heavy just plain water was.

When he went back out again, John had fallen asleep right where he sat, leaning against the porch railing—worn out. Even Massie looked out at him mournfully from under the porch, shaking ashes from his ears.

Luke looked at the sad black rubble of the barn. He could still hear, in his mind, John calling him . . . and he could see himself running off in the opposite direction. What if he had returned to find the house, too, burned flat, or John or his mother hurt . . . or worse.

As John said, it did no good to be sorry. Being sorry didn't build the barn back. John was right—he was undependable. Look at all the things he had done—how many times he had gone chasing skunks when he promised not to, the time he found Tokala and stayed in the woods till full dark, scaring his mother; the time he ran off like a child and left the well cover off; and now, when he was needed and knew he was needed, to run off again just because he was tired of work.

They would be better off, he decided, without him. Without him to worry about, or feed, or look out for.

He would run away, now, while everyone was asleep.

He rolled extra clothes into a bundle and packed a lunch of bread and cheese. There was half an apple pie on the sink board and he almost added that too, but it didn't seem right.

It might be, he thought, a long time before he ever saw the cottage again, or the empty fox pen behind the remains of the barn, or the garden patch that had used up so much time and hard work. Then there were all the secret trails winding back through the woods, places he had gone with Pa. And somewhere there was To-kala, poking his nose out from cover. If there were time he would like to visit all those places again. But there was only time to make one visit. He could not leave, forever, without saying good-by to the Princess.

He thought, too, about taking Massie; the dog would be a lot of comfort and company on the long journey, wherever it happened to take him. But that would leave his mother alone whenever John happened to be away.

It had been scary rowing across the lake at night, as he did the first time, but it was blazing hard work rowing across in the heat of the day. He could feel his face, hardened as it was to sun, tighten with sunburn. The sun on the water hurt his eyes too. He wondered if maybe John or his mother might wake up and find his note and come looking for him. They could see him, out here in the middle of the lake, but there would be no way for them to get to him.

He had puzzled a long time over that note before it was written to his satisfaction. He had wanted them to understand that he was not running away like a child, because his feelings were hurt or because he was mad; but because he was ashamed and didn't want to be a bother to them any more. It was a shame that he couldn't write a note for Massie, too. Massie wouldn't understand; he would go nosing around the house and under the furniture looking for Luke. But Massie would forget about him in time.

And Tokala might come looking once or twice, but he would forget even sooner—maybe already had.

They would all forget him. John could say, in case anyone ever asked, "We don't know what became of him. He just went off one day, and he's never been seen or heard from since."

By the time he got to the cool green trees on the other side of the lake, the sun was low on the horizon and Luke had the uncomfortable feeling that he would arrive at the lodge of the Princess right at her supper-time, which was about the worst kind of bad manners.

He peered up the path and, sure enough, he saw smoke—maybe from a stove or campfire—so he squatted down back from the path under a big tree and ate some of his bread and cheese. It tasted good and he didn't let himself think about the half an apple pie home on the sink board. Nor would he let himself think about what John and his mother might be having for supper. He finished off with a few swallows of lake water to wash things down, and then, concluding that the Princess was probably through eating, he went on up the path.

She was sitting cross-legged in the clearing behind her house, her blanket wrapped around her and, to his astonishment, smoking a pipe. Of course he knew Indians smoked pipes, but he never thought about the Princess smoking one. Then, too, he remembered something about everyone around a council fire sharing a pipe, as a token of friendship. He hoped to goodness the Princess wouldn't offer to share her pipe with him; he didn't know how it would go on top of the bread and cheese and the long row and the hot sun. But of course if she offered to share, why then he must do it.

She didn't take any notice of him, although he knew she saw him standing there, and after a minute he sat down cross-legged across from her. She had to speak first, he knew. That was proper ceremony.

"Lu-kas Mitch-ell," she said at last in her slow way. "Boy-who-rows-by-night," and she chuckled.

"I came to say good-by," Luke said.

"No snake-bite?"

"No. Fire this time. Our barn burned down."

The Princess grunted. It was a wonder, Luke thought, how nothing ever seemed to surprise her.

"Mostly on account of me, too. Just like the snake-bite. They called me to come help with the water buckets, but I didn't come, and Mother and John couldn't keep 'em coming fast enough."

"You did not hear?"

"I heard, all right. Just didn't come." He sighed. "Just didn't come help put out the fire. Just didn't see to the well cover, just didn't do my chores, just couldn't leave the skunks alone."

The Princess puffed on her pipe.

"So I came to say good-by. I'm running away."

She looked at him now, with some spark of interest in her deep black eyes. "To where?"

"Why . . . to somewhere else, I guess. Just away."
He kicked a loose stone toward the fire. "Never coming back."

The Princess nodded, swaying back and forth. "The young men of my tribe also run away. They run away alone, away from the lodge, away from the camp, back into the forest to where they can no longer see the smoke of the campfires, to where they are alone. All alone."

That was news to Luke, and welcome news. Once or twice while he was in the middle of the lake—half-hoping somebody would see him, maybe, from the shore—he had wondered if it wasn't a childish thing to run away.

"They take a knife, a hatchet, two days' supply of grain."

"I've got bread and cheese," he said.

"They stay away many days, many nights. They grow lean with hunger and weary with running. And then, if they are strong and brave, the Great Spirit will speak to them in a Medicine Dream. And when they return they sit at the council fire with the wise men of the tribe, and tell what they have seen and what they have learned. Sometimes they tell of drought, of many days to come without rain, and then the tribe sets by a larger store of food in preparation. Sometimes they tell of great wars to be fought, and then the braves paint and sound the war drums and call on the Great Spirit for victory. It was in a

Medicine Dream that my many-times grandfather, Massasoit, first learned of the coming of the White Man.

"He went far into the forest, seeking that place where sky and earth meet, and he was away more days than fingers can count but he could never come to that place, until at last he fell, worn with hunger and with running always to where the sun went down. And the Great Spirit spoke to him there in his dream and said that no man would ever come to that place, for it belonged to the Great Spirit, who sent the sun up each day and called it back at night. But for his trial, the Great Spirit gave my many times grandfather strong medicine and told him that the pale-faced ones would come in a boat with wings.

"When the tribe heard this they laughed and said it was no medicine dream but a madness come out of hunger."

"But they did come," Luke said.

"They came, in a boat with wings, and it was all as the Great Spirit said. Then all knew how strong a medicine had been given my many-times grand-father."

"Did it ever happen," Luke asked, "that a brave would run away and be hungry and do everything right, and still not have a dream?"

The Princess nodded. "They would try again. Sometimes the very old men, when it was time for them to die, would go alone into the forest still one last time, seeking a Medicine Dream."

Luke sat silently, watching the smoke from the Princess' pipe curl up around her white head. He wasn't sure he understood about this dream. "Does a voice speak?" he asked finally. "Does it speak words, like people do?"

"If the dream is a big dream and the medicine is very strong, the Great Spirit speaks as a man, in the words of a man. Or he may speak in the voice of wind through the trees. Or he may come disguised, as a sign. He may come as a deer. He may come"—she looked closely at Luke—"as a red fox. He once came to a brave of my tribe as a fish, in a time when there was no rain and the earth baked and game fled and even the waters were empty. This brave went seeking strong medicine to help my people and he came upon a small trickle of water between two rocks and there he saw this fish, silver and shining in the sun, and this fish leaped high in the air and back as fish do in running waters, though there was little water in the stream. And the brave knew this was the sign he sought and he returned and told the tribe. And all the young men went out upon the lake in canoes and found enough fish to feed all the tribe through the dry time."

Night had fallen as they sat there; the moon was high over the pines, and the campfire had burned down to a bare flicker. Now the Princess set her pipe on the ground and stood up, drawing her blanket tight around her. She was plainly ready to go to bed. Luke didn't like to think about starting off now, in the dark of night. He would like to curl up right here by the remains of the campfire, where things were still familiar to him, and start to run away tomorrow morning. Probably the Princess wouldn't mind, but on the other hand, probably the Princess would think that was a mighty poor way to start, for a person who aimed to run away forever.

"Well," he stood up too. "I better get started."

"Huh," the Princess grunted.

It was a funny thing, saying good-by forever to an Indian Princess. Anyone else would cry and carry on, but the Indians didn't do it that way. Pa had once told him that when an Indian died, he was never spoken of again, even by his closest kin. At the time Luke thought that was sensible, but now he did wish the Princess would make some little kind of fuss. After

91

all, she would never see him again, and *never* was a mighty long time.

He walked off down the path toward the shore and when he looked back she was still standing in the cleared place beside the house, and she did raise one arm out in front of her, which was a way of greeting and, he guessed, a way of farewell.

chapter 6

He had planned to row back again across the lake, leave the boat, and then strike out for Middleboro and wherever else seemed like a good place to go. But now he saw that that plan was downright foolish. First of all, if John or his mother saw him, that would be an end to the whole thing. Second, somebody in Middleboro might spot him and send him home. On the whole, it seemed like a better plan to row up the shore on this side till he came to a likely-looking place and beach the boat there; hide it under loose brush and

93

maybe mark it somehow, so if anyone ever found it, they would know whose boat it was and how it came to be there.

He had gone quite a distance, and was well beyond the wide curve of the lake. Though the shore looked pretty much the same all along, with trees and spotty patches of beach, it was new territory and Luke felt that he had truly left home behind him and was on his way. He was tired, too; tired enough to fall asleep on the hard bottom of the boat without wishing for his soft bed at home. He drifted in close to shore where a willow tree dipped its supple branches into the water, and he looped two branches together through the iron ring at the prow end of the boat and knotted them. Then he rolled the extra shirt in a ball on the bottom of the boat and used it for a pillow. The boat swung easily in a half-circle, and the lapping ripples of the lake lifted it gently and he fell sound asleep.

When Luke woke up, the sun was high in the sky, shining through the leaves of the willow tree like golden lace on the water, and he took off all his clothes and dropped over the side of the boat. He thought, as he often had, that this was the only kind of bath worth bothering with; a hundred times better than heating up water for hours on the stove and then filling up the tub that wasn't big enough anyway. And as for soap—well, he could get along without soap.

He measured out a portion of the bread and cheese and ate it slowly, to make it seem like more, and then untied the boat and started off again. He kept a sharp eye out for a place to go ashore, but there didn't seem even to be any beach along here. The woods came straight down to the water and there wouldn't be any way to hide the boat. Once or twice he watched deer come out of the forest and dip their heads to drink and then, when they saw him, bound back to cover. He saw rabbits, too, and a whole family of raccoons lined up at the water's edge washing their funny white faces.

It was so pleasant, drifting along in the boat with no chores to do or think about doing, that he didn't know why he hadn't run away before. He had thought about it once, when Pa died, but the funny thing was that he planned then to run away *to* the cottage and live there all by himself. Now here he was running in the opposite direction.

One thing, he had never thought running away would be so lonesome. He didn't so much miss people, for there were no people outside of family around the cottage anyway, but he missed Massie, or Tokala

—some live thing to talk to. Once or twice he called out to animals on the shore, but the sound of his voice only scared them away. Probably they had never seen a human before; there were no towns along this side of the lake and no cottages either.

Now that Luke thought about it, maybe he hadn't been so smart to run away in this direction: the bread and cheese would run out soon, and before that happened he wanted to be someplace where he could pick up a job of work, doing chores maybe for someone at one of the farms outside Middleboro.

He had no way to calculate how far along the lake shore he had come, but it was surely far enough that he could strike out for the opposite shore. One thing was sure—he wasn't going to get very far if he spent much more time rowing back and forth across this lake. He remembered all his worries, the first of the summer, about how to get John to row him across and that seemed pretty funny now, and long ago. It just went to prove that you never knew what you could do till you had to.

At least it was a cloudy day. He hadn't realized that until he tried to figure the time and then he saw that the sky was leaden and gray without even the least bit of sunshine, which made the rowing a lot easier. Even so, he was getting pretty tired of the boat. A boat was fine for a while, but it was a limited kind of a thing and he was more than ready to tie it up and stretch his legs and go on foot.

There was a big hollow place, too, in the pit of his stomach, and he looked at the remains of his lunch. He had divided it into five portions and, by rights, he had already eaten that day's portion, but even if he lasted out the five days he wasn't so sure the bread and cheese would. It already looked a little mashed. It would be silly to go hungry now and then have the food spoil on him, and it *would* be a hard pull across the lake.

He took one more portion, chewing it very slowly. At home his mother always said, "Be thankful for what you have" . . . if you don't have fried chicken, be thankful for potatoes; if you don't have strawberry shortcake, be thankful for a glass of milk.

"I could be a lot more thankful if this bread and cheese would turn into a pie," he thought. But his mother was right—it was better than nothing.

He let the boat drift while he ate and he was surprised at how far along it had come. He was surprised, too, to see that the wind had started up, and started up strong. He had to pull hard at the oars to turn himself into the middle of the lake and now, way off in the distance, he could hear thunder. Raindrops began to spatter against the boat—no gentle rain-on-the-roof, either; they were big heavy drops and the wind drove them stinging against his face.

Now the lake, which had been smooth as glass not ten minutes before, began to churn and toss around him, throwing up whitecaps and knocking the boat from side to side. It wasn't any use to try rowing, so he put the oars up in the locks and braced himself against the sides of the boat to keep it steady and upright.

He saw now, too late, what had happened. He had let himself get caught out away from shore, in the middle of a lake squall.

"They come up that fast," John had told him. "You may think to yourself that it looks a little stormy and the very next minute you're in the middle of it, and it's a lucky man who can ride one out."

It was the main reason his mother never wanted him rowing very far out, and Pa had told a hundred stories of people who got caught in a lake squall and were never seen or heard of again. "It's like the ocean," Pa said, "with breakers as high as a man's head, and white foam flying through the air, and the water tossing logs and sticks . . . and boats . . . around, like Massie with a bone."

Luke had never seen the ocean except calm and

peaceful in Plymouth Bay, but he had only to look around him to know what Pa meant. The water wasn't the clear blue-green that he knew; it was gray and black and angry.

The rain, coming in sheets of water, shut out all signs of shore or trees or anything but the tossing water. He felt a big swell lift the boat up and carry it, almost on the crest of a wave, and then set it down

99

again as if the boat were no more than a chip of wood. Luke knew that if he were on the other end of such a wave he wouldn't stand a chance, and he tried to look around and spot danger coming, but there were so many waves in so many directions that he couldn't guard against them all. A wall of spray and foam burst over him, turning the boat almost around on itself, and one oar pulled loose from the lock and floated away in the backwash of the wave.

The thunder was close now; it seemed to echo all around him and boom through the depths of the lake as well, as if thunder in the sky set off more thunder in the water to slam against the sides of the boat. Lightning ripped overhead, forking down into the lake.

If he had had time he would have worried about that, too, for he knew the worst place in the world to be was on water in a thunderstorm. But the way he was fixed, it looked to Luke as if it was just a case of which would get him first—the waves or the lightning.

Just then, off to the side, he saw the shape of trees through the blowing rain. He could hardly believe that he had got to the other side—maybe he had just been tossed back toward the shore he put out from.

He tried to back-water with the one oar, thinking to turn the boat straight toward the line of trees, but between the wind and the lake swell one oar was no good. All kinds of shore debris—twigs and logs and branches—were floating around him and he tried to use the oar to catch one fair-sized branch. The branch, he thought, would do for another oar long enough to get to the trees.

Too late, he saw a wall of water coming right at him: it was as high as White Banks, as high as the Sentinel Pine. He could hardly see up to its white-foamed edge before it broke above and around him, tossing the boat up and over.

Luke came up sputtering and surprised to find himself still alive, at least for the moment. The wave had really done him a service by throwing him closer to the line of trees, which he could see clearly now. But the boat was gone, thrown somewhere by that wall-high wave—no use to wonder where.

Pa had taught him to swim, had taught him to take long, smooth, easy strokes, but that was in a friendly lake. Now he scrabbled along to shore the best he could, choking and swallowing and spitting up water.

It was just like rowing over the lake the first time:

it had to be done, and so he did it. Now he had to get to the shore and out of this boiling storm, and so, again, he did it and pulled himself up, at last, to lie on a gnarled tangle of tree roots, growing half in the water.

He took a minute to catch his breath and then stumbled back from the shore into the woods, back from the pounding waves to where the trees would afford some shelter. He was wet through and his shoes made sloshy, sucking noises when he walked. He sat down on a bed of soggy pine needles, shivering all over. He found bumps and bruises here and there from knocking against the boat and his whole left leg was scrape-burned from clambering up onto the tree roots, but none of that mattered, now that he was on land. He leaned his head back against a pine tree, just to rest for a minute before he would start back through the woods to find some people or a farm or a town or something.

He didn't doze long; it was still daylight when he opened his eyes and looked around.

The storm was over. Way, way off he could hear the faintest rumbles of thunder. The lake was settling back again, though it was still covered with whitecaps and small rippling waves. The whole thing put him in mind of a girl in the school at Middleboro, who would throw the wildest tantrums about nothing at all and then—that quick—she would get over it and smile as if to say, "Well, I stirred things up good and proper!" That was just the way the lake looked to him.

The sky had cleared too, and now he could see around a little, with no curtains of rain to hide things.

He could see now that he wasn't on the opposite shore of the lake at all.

He was on Minitik Island.

He was on Minitik Island, without a boat, and night coming on fast.

Run! he thought. I'll run! But where to? There was no running away from an island. Whatever ghosts and haunts there were here, he would have to face up to them.

For the first time he wished Pa hadn't been so obliging with stories about Minitik Island. It was one thing to shiver and shake in front of the fire in your own house where you could reach out and touch your own walls; it was something else again to stand all alone on the shore of a spirit-haunted place while darkness fell and wind whispered through the trees . . . if it was wind.

Something he had never realized before was the friendliness and warmth of light: the kitchen light over the big table where he could read in the evenings, the coal-oil lantern when the electricity failed, the lights shining from the windows when you happened to get home at dusk, the flame and flicker of the Princess' campfire last night . . . was it just last night?

Later on there would be the moon, of course, but he didn't know what the moonlight might reveal, deep in the shadows of bushes and the hollows of trees. It might show him things better left unseen.

It was a funny feeling to be on an island, and it was a funny feeling, too, to be where nobody else had ever been before. Even fishermen skirted way around Minitik, unwilling to trust their luck anywhere close to haunted waters.

No fishermen, no towns or people . . . how would he ever get off the island? The boat was gone, and with it his extra clothes and the last remains of food. It wouldn't do any good to call, for there was nobody to hear him.

But, he thought, if he could build a fire someone might see the smoke and come looking. Then, too, if he had a fire he could get warm. And he might be able to catch some fish and cook them. So the principal thing he needed was a fire, but he knew that was useless to think about now with everything water-soaked. He would have to wait till morning, till the sun came up to dry things out.

He gathered an armload of soggy pine branches from under the trees at the water's edge and made a bed for himself. Dry pine branches made a nice springy place to lie, and even wet ones were better than the tree roots with knobs and knuckles of wood to dig into him everywhere so he couldn't move. The moon was coming up now, shining pale and cold through drifting clouds, and Luke followed its light in all directions, but there was nothing to see: nothing hiding in the brush, nothing springing out at him . . . yet.

It was different from the woods at home; here there were no animal sounds, only the steady drip-drip of rain still falling from the trees. Now and then a breath of wind moved through the trees, creaking their branches together, and then there would be a sudden shower of raindrops on his face.

He couldn't sleep, not just because of the damp and all his bumps and bruises, but because everything was so strange. He was waiting to see what mysterious things moved on Minitik Island on a rainy, cloud-dimmed night. The trees were so heavy that they held the moisture of the rain, and made a low ground mist that spread in all directions, so you could

105

almost believe that it was a fog island, as some people said.

He lay, wondering what the secret of the island
might be. He wondered if maybe someone had come
close to the shore once—maybe on a misty night just
like this one—and had seen a gnarled old tree and
took it for a haunt. There was such a tree just ahead

of him; it was bent and twisted and its branches looked like arms in the moonlight. But it had to be more than that. A boy might be frightened by such a sight, but not a grown person. And it was grown people who said that Minitik was haunted. Even Pa would never come near the island, and Pa wasn't afraid of anything.

There was a quick flutter of sound off to the left and then a deep, hollow drum sound that nearly scared Luke skinless. He sat bolt upright and grabbed a tree branch, though what good that would be he didn't know.

The moon cleared the clouds for a minute and Luke saw a big green granddaddy bullfrog sitting on a tree root, his throat swelled up like mumps as he croaked again, and then, in two hops, bounded off toward the water.

Luke felt better; he knew there were all kinds of things around him that he couldn't see or hear, and it was a comfort to have one live thing in the neighborhood. First thing in the morning, he decided, he would see about a fire, and contrive some kind of fishing pole. He dug deep into his pockets and turned them out, though he knew there was nothing there except his knife. Everything else had floated away in the storm: the pieces of string and stray seeds from

planting, his lucky piece Indian-head penny—that
was what got him through the storm, he knew—and
the odd nails. He fell asleep thinking about those
nails and all he could do with them: make a fishhook,
or piece together some kind of raft. But they were
gone, and all he had were his two hands and a ten-
cent pocketknife.

The sun woke him—a high, hot sun, he saw thank-
fully—hot enough to dry out wood, and his clammy
clothes. He hung his pants and shirt over the tree
branches where the sun could get at them and he
gathered a whole armload of little twigs and spread
those, too, in the sun where they'd get tinder-dry and
be good for a fire.

He was so hungry he thought his stomach must
be smack up against his backbone, and if he shut his
eyes all he could see was that half an apple pie on
the sink board at home. If you haven't got apple pie,
he told himself, be thankful . . . for what? He didn't
have anything to be thankful for, except that he had
lived through the storm and lived through a night on
Minitik.

He found a good stick for a fishing pole, and pulled
wild vines from around the trees to use for a line. He
realized now that he should have dug for worms the
night before, but a worm wasn't much use without

some kind of hook and he wished again for all those good nails, lost somewhere in the lake.

The storm had left a water line of debris—mostly twigs and small stones and limp mounds of water grasses and leaves—but he did find one possible substitute for a hook . . . a chunk of heavy glass with a broken splinter edge. The sun shining down through the water made the glass sparkle and wink—perfectly good bait, Luke decided, which saved him the job of digging for worms. And if the hook end didn't work —well, the Princess had said they used to catch fish by hand.

As he sat, waiting for a bite, he kept looking out over the lake just in case somebody might come along, though he didn't have much hope of that. It appeared to Luke as if he might be on this island from now on and he would have to plan accordingly. He would need some kind of shelter, probably a tree house. And once he did get a fire started, he would have to find some way of keeping it alive. If there should be a shallow cave or a rock ledge he could build his fire there, where the rain couldn't put it out or the wind scatter it.

He didn't know what he'd do for clothes as the years went by; his shirt and pants wouldn't last forever. The Indians used deerskins, but there weren't any deer on Minitik Island. He hadn't seen any animal signs at all, but there was no telling what animals might lurk back in the interior of the island . . . maybe animals he had never heard of before.

One thing was sure: he would have to go see. There must be berries and nuts, maybe squirrels and rabbits . . . the very thought of food made him dizzy.

Suddenly he caught a glint of silver in the water. It was a fish, finally attracted by the shiny glass. The fish swam all around the line while Luke sat as still as if he were a tree stump, hardly daring to breathe. He saw the fish nibble, or try to nibble, and then swim around the glass bait again.

So the hook wasn't going to work. Somehow, without moving that line even a hair, Luke would have to wiggle himself down to the water and snatch the fish out. Slowly he transferred the pole from one hand to the other and leaned down. He didn't know how much fish could see of colors, but the sun was shining in such a way that glass sent off ruby-red sparks in all directions, and he thought that if he were a fish he would be content just to look at such a pretty sight for a while—long enough, say, to get caught.

Swish! It happened so fast that Luke wasn't sure for a minute whether he had him or not till he saw the fish flapping around on the shore. He must have

flung it right over his head, and there it lay . . . supper!
Wait'll I tell the Princess! he thought, forgetting for
a minute that he would never see the Princess again
to tell her.

He cleaned the fish and then carried his dry sticks
to where he had slept the night before. Pa had showed
him how to make a fire by rubbing sticks together over
a pile of tinder, but either he didn't pay close enough
attention or he wasn't doing it right, because no matter how hard he rubbed he couldn't get a spark. It
was terrible to be hungry and have nothing to eat,
but it was six times worse to be hungry and have
something to eat and no way to cook it.

He knew he had to get something in his stomach
or he would go all dauncy. That was his mother's
word for the weak trembles, when your head went
fuzzy and you saw double and lost your strength. Luke
didn't want to get in any such fix as that.

Plainly there was nothing to eat here, but there
must be berrybushes back in the island, back from
the shore in among all the tall dark trees. There were
probably other things too, but he didn't like to think
about what.

He started slowly, picking his way. There was nothing like a path, just thick underbrush and fallen trees
to climb over. The forest seemed to close in behind

111

him and with every step he took, the thought ran through his head, "No one has ever been here before. No one has ever been here before." The only sound was the high-up flutter of birds—at least he hoped they were birds.

With every step, too, he realized more and more how hopeless an idea it was to think he could survive here on the island, alone and without any tools to help him. Somehow he would have to get off, or get somebody to take him off, or build some kind of raft. If he only had those nails! It was a wonder, he thought, the things you took for granted: nails, and fishhooks, and rope and dry clothes, and breakfast . . . and fire.

If he ever got home again he would never complain about carrying wood; he would carry wood from here to Boston just for the pleasure of striking a match and seeing it burst into flame. If he ever got home . . . he knew now how wrong he had been to run away. That was no way to show he was truly sorry about the barn burning and the well cover and all the other things he did wrong. The worst thing of all was to run away, and leave John to do all the chores. If he could just get back and show them that he really wasn't so worthless and undependable . . . if he could just ever get back!

"If I could only get back!" He looked up, startled at the sound of his own voice.

And there, in the crotch of a tree not a foot away from him, was a face, painted red and yellow; and below it, imbedded in the trunk of the tree, a hatchet, its handle sticking out as if an unseen hand had stuck it there and was waiting to draw it out again!

chapteR 7

Then Luke ran! Hungry or not, dauncy or not, he ran faster than he ever ran in all his life before, stumbling over roots and brambles, falling down and getting up again. Every time a branch brushed against him he thought it was an arm reaching out to grab him. He could almost feel the sharp edge of that hatchet whiz by his ears. He didn't know in what direction he was headed, and he didn't care till he tripped over a tree stump, knocking the wind out of himself. He lay full length on the ground, his arms over his head, waiting for whatever it was to finish him off.

But nothing happened. And, after the longest minute of his life, he raised his head and looked around. There was nothing behind him, or on either side, but he lay still all the same, straining to hear a footfall in the brush. Hours seemed to go by as he lay there, flat to the ground, afraid to move and afraid not to; afraid, almost, to breathe.

Why had he ever come back into the island? Better to starve to death on shore than to end up here, a hatchet in his head, his scalp missing.

No use to tell himself that a haunt wouldn't want his scalp; he had seen the face, the black eyes glittering at him from the tree. He had seen the tomahawk. Maybe this Indian failed as a warrior when he was alive—never hung a scalp at his belt. Maybe he came to Minitik Island seeking strong medicine to help him, and died here . . . and his spirit stayed on, still hunting his first hair.

Well, he had waited a long time; all these years while sensible people stayed off the island. It wasn't likely he would let Luke get away.

And it might as well be now as later. Besides, Luke thought, "I won't be scalped face down. I'll head for shore and let him pick his own time."

It was slow going; every time he looked behind him, which was every other second, he would trip on something and fall. His knees were scraped and raw, his ankles scratched and bleeding, and once he walked smack into a tree branch.

He thought that was it, that it was all over, and he only thought what a cheat it was for the Indian not to show himself. But it was only a branch, and he was almost sorry. It would be pure pleasure just to lie down on the forest floor and sleep forever.

Still he stumbled on, determined to show some kind of fight no matter how hopeless.

His pants-leg caught in a prickly bush and he leaned over to get it loose, stood up again and looked straight into the cruel staring eyes of the Indian face!

"All right!" he cried, "Come on! Come on!" and braced himself for the blow, the shattering scalp yell.

But the face did not move. There was no rustle of leaves, no crack of twigs. The hatchet, too, was still fast in the tree. He rubbed his eyes, blinked, and looked again.

This face was not a face at all! It was a piece of pudding-stone rock, shaped like a head. There were two hollows for eyes and the paint that looked so bright when he first saw it was dark now in the fading light. It was some kind of plant stain, streaked along the cheeks of the rock face. The head of the hatchet was stone too, chiseled to a fine edge and fastened to the handle with what looked like leather thongs. When he touched it, the thongs parted like dust, leaving the head still buried in the tree and the wooden handle in his hand.

By all rights, he knew he should have been struck down when he touched the hatchet. These things belonged to the spirit of Minitik Island; they weren't put there for a boy to meddle with.

Why were they there, though? A stone face and a hatchet, propped in a tree, as if an Indian brave stood there on guard. What was there to guard?

He looked around. The trees here were scrubbier, almost as if the whole area had been cleared once, long ago, and had not yet grown back. There was a wide circle of this kind of sparse vegetation, rimmed all around with tall, ancient pines. It was not big enough to be a camping place, which was what he thought at first.

Why would someone—Indians, he guessed—go to all the trouble to clear this land on a deserted island, and then go off and leave it? Maybe, he thought, and shuddered, it was a torture place for captives . . . that would be a good reason for Minitik Island to be haunted! But then surely there would be a tall pine, left growing in the middle . . . for a stake.

He walked along, kicking at the pine needles, until he stubbed his toe against a rock. It was not an ordinary rock, but a hatchet head like the one in the tree, its edge chiseled sharp, and there were lines along the back of it as though ties or thongs had worn into the stone. Luke thought it would be a useful tool for him, and he looked around for any others.

There were no more hatchet handles, but he found stone arrowheads scattered all through the pine needles, and a scoop-shaped thing of reddish clay that might have been a bowl once, being hollowed out in the middle. He used it for a hand shovel, to dig down into the sandy soil, and there under the ground he found more things: arrowheads and clay dishes and bowls, another hatchet head, long slivers of bone with holes bored at one end—needles, for sewing hides. He found bone knives, the edges carved as sharp as his mother's butcher knife. He found leather or hide pouches which fell apart as he touched them—it was a perfect treasure chest of tools, buried here.

But it didn't make sense! The Indians never buried their implements and weapons, unless . . . He sat back on his heels, and a cold shiver ran up his spine.

Night had fallen as he dug, and now the full moon

shone bright as day over the forest, down into the hole in the ground—down into the grave.

For that was what it was . . . had to be. When an Indian died, his things were buried with him: his bow and arrows, his tomahawk, his eating bowl. He looked again at the pile of bone needles. Some of them, he realized now, were too big to be needles, too thick to be anything but what they really were—skeleton bones.

This was the burial ground of many braves—perhaps all killed in the same battle and buried together with their weapons, their resting place marked and guarded by the stone face in the tree.

Now he understood the secret of Minitik Island. Of course no one ever came here—the Indians did not return to their dead, but left them to the care of the Great Spirit. And so the legend must have grown —that Minitik Island was haunted. And so it was: haunted by the memory of these Indian warriors.

If ever he was going to be scared, this was the time, but somehow Luke felt more comfortable than any time since he landed on the island. Pa always said, "People are most afraid of the unknown," and wasn't that just the way with Minitik? Now that he knew the secret of the island, it was all different. Besides, Luke felt perfectly friendly about the Indians; they were bound to be warriors of the Princess' tribe, and she was his friend.

It suddenly occurred to him that the Princess might not even know about the burial ground; it was so old, likely before her time. But he could take her some of the arrowheads and the bone knives and things and tell her about the stone face and the skeletons, and he could tell her how the land had been cleared and what a peaceful place it was generally. That would be a present!

Then, too, he would probably be famous—the first person to find out the truth of Minitik Island. People would even point to him on the street, and John—well, John might forgive him a lot of things, considering all he'd done and seen.

He slept in the burial ground that night, too tired to wander any farther. In the morning he made a poke of his shirt and loaded it with one of every kind of thing he had dug up, and he filled up the hole and smoothed pine needles over the top, so that everything was just the same as he had found it. As he walked away from the burial place the trees filled in behind him and covered any sign of what was there.

Almost immediately he came upon a big patch of wild berry bushes. He must have gone right by them yesterday and didn't even notice. The berries were only about half ripe, but three big handfuls made a big difference to his stomach. He thought about the Indians who would be gone for days and days with only a handful of grain and he was ashamed of his own weakness . . . ashamed, too, that he had thought even for a minute of staying here forever. No Indian who ever lived would let himself get stuck on an island and not even try to get away.

"Ho, Mr. Fisherman," he sang, "I know you mighty well . . ." He sang that all the way through, and "Blue Tail Fly" and "Low Bill, the Whaling Man." "Low Bill" had twenty-three verses and he sang it through twice before he saw the gleam of water between the trees and came out on the edge of the island.

It was a different edge; there was no sign of his fish or his pile of tinder wood or the heavy old tree with the big roots. Here there was a narrow strip of sandy beach, with a stand of rushes right off shore. And there was something else.

Caught in the rushes, bobbing up and down on the water, was an oar.

He swam out and brought it in. It was an oar from his own boat; there was the double wrapping of tape Pa had put around the handle, and a notch on one side of the paddle end. For one wild moment he thought the boat, too, might have washed up somewhere on shore, but the chances were it would have broken up in the storm.

He had three choices: he could float with the oar, kicking along behind it, or he could try to swim to shore —both foolish notions, considering the distance, or . . . he could build a raft and use the oar to guide it.

There were plenty of logs scattered up and down the beach, half-buried in sand, blown down by high winds or struck by lightning, and he found two lying a foot or two apart, and a third—a smaller one—propped crosswise over them. It took the rest of that day to pull and push and roll the three logs into a line. Then, by moonlight, he braided long ropes of vine and the tough water rushes and lashed the logs together, one to the other and then all three together at both ends and the middle. His fingers were bloody from the knife-sharp rush edges and sore from digging into the sand under the logs, and his whole hand cramped with pain after forcing the slippery lines into knots.

"A good square knot will never let go," Pa used to say, and Luke certainly hoped he was right. Not that it could matter—a square knot was the only one he knew.

Dawn broke long before he was finished, and the sun was high again when he tied the last knot. He had lost track of the days—three or four . . . maybe a week.

He didn't know how long he had been running away.

Seen in the daylight, it was hard to believe that this pitiful craft had taken so much hard work and time. It wasn't much bigger than the well cover at home, though the middle log, being thin and longer, stuck out fore and aft. Would that overbalance the raft? He didn't know, but he couldn't find any other log that he could move. There were spaces between the logs, too, where it wasn't lashed tight enough, and the whole thing looked like a poorly wrapped package, with the vines going every which way, under and over the logs. But surely it would hold till he got to shore; he wouldn't have to depend on the drift of the water—he had the oar to guide.

He tied the sleeves of his shirt tight around the Indian things and laid the bundle on the raft. Then he got on himself and pushed off with the oar, but the oar only sank in the sand while the raft refused to move. He got off and pushed as hard as he could, but it seemed to be stuck in the sand. He couldn't move it himself— the three logs tied together, small as they were, made the thing too heavy.

He got the scoop-shaped clay bowl from his shirt and, using it and the oar, began to dig a channel in the sand under the logs to float them off. It was hard work —the sand fell back as fast as he dug it out, and the hot

sun made him dizzy. When he stood up, the trees wavered before his eyes and his knees felt weak. There was a good half-day of digging to get the raft free, and then he would be out in the middle of the lake at night. Suppose he fell asleep and lost the oar? Or the raft came apart under him?

The smart thing was to wait: to go find the berry-bushes and get something in his stomach, and spend another night on the island. He could dig the raft out in the cool of morning and then he would be on the lake in daylight, in case he should meet any fishermen.

He found the bushes without any trouble even though he hadn't blazed a trail to them, and he ate slowly, chewing each berry so as to get the most good from it. Then he curled up beside the berry patch and fell asleep to the sound of wind in the pines.

He dreamed of Indians—of Massasoit, of the Princess and all her tribes, and of the braves who were buried all around him. In his dream he was one of them: he had proved himself by going alone onto Minitik Island and staying there many days, living on berries. He had built a raft—though in his dream it was a light, slim birch canoe—and he returned at last to the tribe and told all that he had seen: the stone face and the hatchet. And the old men of the tribe nodded their heads over the council fire and said it was a sign that Minitik Island was meant to be their burial place, and secret to them. Then the Princess sang her song about him—Chasatonga—and gave him an eagle feather to wear in his headband.

When Luke woke up he could hardly make himself believe that it was all a dream, that he was Lucas Mitchell instead of an Indian boy with a feather headdress and moccasins on his feet and a Medicine Dream to tell about. As he dug away under the raft he pretended it was a canoe, and when it came loose and floated free out onto the lake he almost hated to climb aboard.

Not until he had paddled all the way around the curve of the lake and Minitik Island was gone from sight, did he begin to think about home; what his mother and John would say, what Massie would do, and other, more practical things like bread and butter and potatoes and crackly fried chicken.

He got the trick of steering the raft—and it was a trick, for the logs, being tied so loosely, tended to float free of each other. He had to watch not to get a foot caught between them, and he steercd in close to shore in case the raft did break up.

It held together all the way to Indian Shore and then, a few yards below the Princess' camp, he ran onto submerged tree roots. He felt the jolt and just had time to hop ashore before the vines parted and his raft floated away in three directions.

It didn't matter now, this close, though he had hoped to go back across the lake and home on the raft. Maybe he could build another raft, or maybe the Princess would teach him how to make a birch canoe. As he walked along the beach and then up the path to the house he smelled a wonderful smell of food cooking, a rich meaty smell, and his knees nearly buckled under him with hunger. He had to stop on the path and get himself in hand, so he wouldn't come weak and shaking to the campfire.

Then he walked slowly to where the Princess sat, holding his shirt bundle in front of him in both hands.

chapter 8

The Princess was watching a big black cook-pot hanging on three stakes over her campfire. As she stirred it with a long-handled spoon the fragrant steam drifted in Luke's direction and made his mouth water so that he had to swallow over and over again, hard.

"You have come back," she said at last, and he nodded.

"Will you eat?" She ladled a big plateful, put a piece of hard bread on top, and handed it to him.

It was a stew—rabbit, he thought—with big chunks

130

of meat and firm potatoes swimming in dark brown gravy. He had to force himself to eat it slowly, as if he didn't care, really, whether he ate or not, and when he had finished every scrap and wiped the bowl clean with the bread, the Princess spoke again.

"Men look for you," she said. "Many men come in boats. One tall man, with yellow hair, called Ja-han." She made two syllables of the name.

"My brother," Luke nodded.

"They came to me."

"What did you tell them?"

"That you were gone into the forest." She squinted at him. "It is strange to me that so many men did not find one boy-who-rows-by-night."

"Where did they look?" Luke asked.

She waved her arm in a wide gesture above her head. "In these woods." Then she pointed across the lake. "In the far-side woods."

Luke pointed too, down the lake, toward the island. "I was in different woods," he said and then, sitting very straight, "I was on Minitik Island."

"Ah-h-h-h."

He watched closely to see if that meant anything particular, but the Princess' eyelids did not even flicker.

"The Spirit Island," she said. "A boat was found in broken pieces," she counted on her fingers, "two days.

132

And now they do not look any more. A woman came, with sad eyes, to see this boat. And now they do not look any more.

Luke felt as if someone had hit him a hard blow in the stomach. They thought he was dead! His mother and John . . . they thought he was dead! Somehow, that thought hadn't occurred to him.

"It was in the storm," he said. "The boat turned over and got swept away. But I found an oar . . ."

"Boy!" she stopped him, and then leaned forward. "Boy . . . tell me about the Spirit Island. Tell me of that."

He started to spill out the whole story, as you would any big thing you had to tell, but then he remembered where he was and whom he was talking to. He remembered his dream, and he stood up by the campfire and told his story as the Indians did, acting it out for all to see.

He showed how he swam to shore, and pointed to his bumps and scrapes. He told about catching the fish —the Princess chuckled at that, her eyes crinkling up when he went Swish! He made signs of hunger and fear when he saw the stone face. Then, saving the best till last, he skipped to the part about the raft, and showed how he pushed the logs together and tied them and dug in the sand to free them.

133

Then he went back to the part about the face in the tree and showed again how he had run at first, then how he returned and dug in the sand and what he found, and finally he made great sweeping gestures to show that he had covered the grave over and left it all as he had found it.

And then, at last, he opened his shirt bundle and laid it on the ground before the Princess, and sat down across from her.

She examined first one thing and then another, running the arrowheads through her fingers, hefting the hatchet head and testing its sharp edge on her thumb. She made curious, sewing movements with the bone needles. Then she laid all the things out in a row before her and sat looking at them for a long time.

Luke wondered if she might be angry at him for disturbing the grave. "I only took one of each thing," he said, "except the arrowheads because there were so many. And I covered it all over again." He thought of something else. "I didn't bring any of the . . . bones. That wouldn't be right."

"A-i-e-e-e," the Princess said, and then she began to chant, swaying back and forth. It was a high, reedy song she sang—a death song. Her fingers returned again and again to the stone implements, touching the worn places where thongs had been, cutting the air with the bone knives.

When she was finished Luke asked, "Did you know? About the island, I mean, and the burial ground?"

"When I was a child," the Princess said, "there was a song of many braves who died in battle on these shores and were buried together in a place apart."

"A place apart," Luke echoed.

She sighed. "I have forgotten the song. There were many songs, when I was a child."

"When I was on the island," he said, "I had a dream. I dreamed I was the first person ever to be there, and I found the stone face and all and I came back and told about it. In the dream, I was an Indian," he added, and then, "I don't guess, though, you could really call that a Medicine Dream."

"Huh," the Princess grunted. Then, without another word, she got up and went into the house.

Luke kicked at the glowing campfire. He thought about what the Princess had said: that nobody was looking for him any more, that they thought he was dead, drowned in the lake. He could just stay here if he wanted to: live with the Princess, and hunt and fish, trap skunks, make a bow and learn to use it. He could find another fox like Tokala; he could kill deer for the hides . . .

Then all of a sudden, with no warning at all, he was homesick. One minute he was half-Indian, trailing game through the forest, and the next minute he couldn't wait to get across the lake, to go up the path to the cottage, to see Massie come flying to meet him—ears up and tail wagging from side to side—to hear his mother and John, to fetch water and carry wood . . . to be home. It was a hurt as real and as bad as being hungry.

The Princess came out again, carrying something in her two hands. It was a thin strip of hide, old and dusty, and the feathers hanging from it were dark with age, their tips broken.

She held it out to him. "For Chasatonga," she said. "I trade . . . for these." She pointed to the pile of stone relics.

"They're yours. I brought them for you." He wanted the headband. "I can't trade for them."

Still she gave it to him. "It is the headpiece of a warrior. I am the last of my tribe, and a Princess. I do not need the headpiece of a warrior." She chuckled. "A boy-who-rows-by-night to the Spirit Island needs the headpiece of a warrior."

Luke held the narrow strip gently. It was soft and there was a faint odor, as if it had been oiled the way John oiled his leather boots to keep them supple.

"Do you know who it belonged to?" he asked.

"It is too old to know. A warrior."

136

"In my dream," Luke said in a whisper, "in my dream, you gave me an eagle feather."

The Princess grunted in her strange, nothing-can-surprise-me-way and then she pointed with the long spoon out toward the lake. "A boat," she said, "a man fishing."

Luke got up slowly. "Then I better go home, if he'll take me across."

"Boy!" she stopped him. "Where will you say that you have been?"

"Why, on Minitik Island, I'll tell them. And about the storm, and all."

"You will not say what is on the island." It wasn't a question.

"You mean the burial ground?"

"If you say, the men who dig will come with shovels. They will take up the bones of my people to make a show. Say only that you were on the island and that it is a swamp and cold, and wet, and nothing more."

Luke had to think a long time. This was the biggest secret he had ever had in his keeping, and it would be easy to say "I promise" now, and forget that promise later when people asked about the island.

"I won't tell," he said finally.

"I don't know when I can come again, now that the

boat's gone." He could build another raft: a better raft, with logs sawed to size and tied with rope, but he didn't know about time. There would be jobs to do at home, to make up for all this time away.

"When the snow falls," the Princess said, "you come. Walk. Over the water."

"Walk over the water?" Luke stared.

"Cold winter." She sniffed the air and nodded. "You bring me turkey for Thanks-giv-ing." Her shoulders shook with laughter under the blanket, laughter at her own joke, and as Luke walked away he determined to do that very thing. Of course he couldn't walk over the lake, but somehow he would contrive to get a turkey there for Thanksgiving.

The man in the boat came right over when Luke hailed him—pulled up his fishing line and just rowed like sixty to the shore.

"Great day in the morning, boy!" he said. "Who are you?"

"I'm Luke Mitchell, and I wonder if you'd mind to take me . . ."

"Luke Mitchell! Great day in the morning! Get in, get in." He almost tipped the boat over in his excitement. "Everybody in these parts been looking for you. Gave you up for dead! My name's Pendleton; work with your brother in to Middleboro. We've been combing the woods for you. . . . Sit right down there, and let me get you home!" He shook his head, as if he couldn't believe Luke was really there. "My, my! Where've you been?"

"I was on Minitik Island."

The man almost dropped his oar. "Great day in . . . No!"

"Yes, sir. I lost my boat in the storm."

"Yes, we found the boat, all smashed over on Indian Shore. That's when we thought . . . your mother thought . . ." He stopped and cleared his throat.

"And I was on the island three days."

"You don't tell me! Well, boy . . . Lukas . . . what's on that island?"

Luke swallowed hard. "Nothing," he said. "Just swamp, like. Snakes," he added, thinking that might serve to keep people away. "Big snakes."

"Bad place, that island," Mr. Pendleton said. "I wouldn't go ten boat-lengths near. They say, you know, it's haunted. Would you say, from your experience, that that's the case? Not that I hold with haunts or ghosts and such, but must be something there."

"I'd say that," Luke agreed. "Might be ghosts, might be anything." He shivered, because it was chilly without his shirt, but Mr. Pendleton took the shiver for something else.

139

"Well, I expect you'll be a right-celebrated boy, for spending three days there, but I don't think many will follow your example. Snakes, you say?"

"Yes, sir."

"And swamp land. Just a good-for-nothing place, that island."

"Yes, sir." Luke crossed his fingers behind his back.

Mr. Pendleton began shouting before they were even close to shore, and his voice echoed up onto the beach. "John!" he called, "Mrs. Mitchell! I've got your boy here! Mrs. Mitchell!"

Massie came first . . . just as Luke had imagined . . . ears flapping and barking and dashing into the water and out. Nothing ever could say welcome like a dog. Then his mother: Luke never knew his mother could run so fast! Her feet fairly flew over the ground, and when she hugged him—little as she was and big as he was—she lifted him right up off his feet, and she was crying. John hugged him too.

Then there was the awfullest racket: with everyone talking at once, and Massie wheeling in and out, jumping on Luke, fairly beside himself. Mr. Pendleton was telling how he found Luke on Indian Shore, and everyone was clamoring to thank him, and to find out where Luke had been, and telling about the smashed-up boat, and where all they had looked, and where in the world had he been? And how people came out from Middle-boro to look, and they asked the Princess, and what she said, and how terrible it was when they found the boat, and where in the world had he been?

Then suddenly his mother clapped her hands. "It's not important where he was, right now," she said. "Later we'll find out. Now you come along with me and have some supper. Just look at the bones of the boy! Sticking right out!" And that was that: they all went up to the cottage.

That supper! Long afterward, Luke could close his eyes and remember that supper. There was chicken . . . a whole chicken, and biscuits and jam and fried pota-toes and beans and tomatoes and eggs and cheese and strawberry pie! And later, when he was telling about having nothing but the half-ripe berries, his mother gasped and her eyes filled up again, and if she didn't fly around and make pancakes! To fill up the holes, she said.

Then, when he was filled up like a balloon, he told them what all he had done. Mr. Pendleton had already heard the story, and he kept putting in things that Luke forgot.

"Right in the middle of that storm! Worst storm in years . . ." he would say, and "Three days! Three days on that island!"

When he told about building the raft, John reached over and clapped him on the shoulder as if he'd done something wonderful. He told a lot about snakes, making it up as he went along. It wasn't so much a lie, he figured, as a protection for the burial ground.

Later, when Mr. Pendleton had left, richer by a pie and two loaves of fresh bread and jars of jam and tomatoes and every other thing his mother could lay her hands on, Luke tried to tell John how sorry he was about running away, and about the barn, and his chores, and everything.

"I'll do better," he said, and meant it.

"I know you will," was all John said, and he meant it too.

His mother came into the bedroom three or four times just to be sure he was comfortable, and he knew she looked in the door twice just to be sure he was there, and he fell asleep to the friendly sound of Massie's tail, thumping on the floor boards beside the bed.

chapter 9

The rest of the summer seemed to fly by. Luke and John, working together, finished the root cellar, and they put up a funny old lean-to of a shed—nothing like the barn that burned, but it would keep the car in out of the cold. They finished the gardens, and there was a good spell of rain after the drought and vegetables fairly popped up. There was half again as much to sell as John had hoped, so that things wouldn't be quite so lean after all, come winter.

And there were glorious, famous days in Middleboro. John said so many people asked about Luke and wanted to hear about him that he couldn't tend to business, so he took Luke along. People crowded around the produce market to see the boy who stayed three days on Minitik Island, and every time Luke told the story, those snakes got bigger and more numerous. It got so he had to watch himself about the snakes, and concentrate more on the storm or the raft building.

He never told about the burial ground. He didn't want to. Right at first, when Mr. Pendleton picked him up on Indian Shore, it had been hard not to tell: he had to bite his tongue so as not to blurt out the whole story. That had been the biggest test of his promise.

Now, he knew if he so much as mentioned dead Indians, there would be a perfect parade of people to Minitik Island: boys, to play hide-and-seek over the graves and fill their pockets with arrowheads; Historical Society people—the "men who dig" the Princess called them—would open trenches in the earth and take up the bones and the stone tools and put them in a museum. They would take down the stone face and the hatchet in the tree and leave nothing there to show what it was. Luke didn't want that to happen. His promise was not just a promise to the Princess, but to himself as well. It was a trust between them, a secret they shared.

144

As it was, the island was safe. The boys said there was no advantage in rowing halfway across the lake to an island where there were no animals and no climbing trees and nothing to do but kill snakes—they could kill snakes at home.

The men said everybody knew the fishing was no good around Minitik.

The women said they wouldn't go to any such swampy place, because of fever and snake-bite.

They all said, "Of course we know there's no such thing as a ghost, no such thing as a haunted island."

That's what they said, but they didn't believe it. Luke could tell. Never mind their excuses, never mind what Luke told them—though, to be perfectly honest, he never said, out and out, that there *wasn't* a haunt on the island—still, people believed there was.

Even John. "No need to go traipsing over to that island," he said one night at supper. "Nothing there of any account: no farm land, no fishing."

"I caught a fish," Luke reminded him.

"Well, no fishing to *speak* of, no hunting. Nothing to go for. Not that I believe there's any ghost or spirit there," he added. "Pure foolishness."

Luke wore his headband to town once or twice, though his mother complained about the dirty place on his forehead, and that set the Historical Society men off. They wanted the headpiece in the very worst way. He heard them talking to John about it.

"It's a valuable thing," they said. "No telling how old it is. It ought to be under glass in the town hall. Why, the boy might lose it."

But all John said was, "It belongs to my brother. It was a gift, and I don't think he aims to give it up."

And of course he was right. Luke wouldn't give it up for anything, but after that he worried for fear he would lose it, or the little children would pull the feathers loose. So finally he put it away in a drawer and only took it out once a month to oil it with John's boot grease and to smooth the turkey feathers out.

And that was how the summer went. He never got to build a raft, but John said he would try to pick up a boat somewhere, cheap, at the end of the season to have for next year.

First frost came, wilting the vegetable vines and covering the ground with a powdered-sugar sift of white.

And school started. Luke had to walk four miles every morning out to the main road where the school bus came to pick him up, but it was no hardship. He got to know the woods as well in autumn as in summer—there was something new to see each morning. There were squirrels chattering at each other as they scurried around picking up nuts to hide away in their secret places, and flocks of birds on their way south, and the trees turning red and gold by the side of the road . . . the four miles wasn't any distance at all.

And then came the first snowfall, early and heavy. School was canceled, and Luke spent the morning shoveling a path around the back door and he shoveled out the fox pen, too. It still stood, behind the lean-to shed, just in case Tokala might remember some day —remember and come back. And he went to the Christmas tree grove, to shake the heavy snow from the young trees, leaving their branches all sparkly. The trees had done well; John said they would have thirty or forty to sell this year.

With that first snowfall winter came . . . and stayed. The hardest winter, people said, in years. But, Luke remembered, the Princess had known that back in August. In the heat of summer, she had known.

Still, he could hardly believe his eyes, to look out the bedroom window one morning and see a solid white glare where the lake had been! He and Massie went down to the shore after breakfast, and Massie, who couldn't get a purchase on the ice, went skittering every which way and yowling, whether from cold or surprise, Luke didn't know. The rushes were frozen straight and stiff, and every few minutes there would be a deep, echoing boom as the ice tightened and cracked from cold. He walked on and on, almost to the middle, before he saw the gleam of water, and then John waved him back from the shore.

"It's almost solid," Luke said. "Will it freeze all the way?"

"They say so," John told him. "In a hard winter the lake is solid ice, two feet thick."

"Shouldn't be long then. When do you think?"

"Oh . . . uncommon cold like this, I should say by Thanksgiving anyway."

So that was what the Princess meant! He could walk over the water, over to Indian Shore.

"I need a turkey," he said that night at supper.

"Well," John laughed, "so do I! Who's giving them away?"

"For the Princess. For Thanksgiving. I told her I'd bring her a turkey, like Pa did."

His mother looked worried. "I don't see how we'll even have a turkey for ourselves this year," she said. "Of course it doesn't really matter. If we don't have turkey, we'll just be . . ."

"Thankful for what we've got," Luke and John finished together.

And, after three days of berries, Luke knew the

truth of that. But he didn't want the turkey for himself.

"Unless . . . ." his mother looked at John, "you'd want to get a wild turkey."

There had been no wild turkeys in the area for years, but this fall a few had been seen.

"I don't know what she'll have for her Thanksgiving dinner if I don't," Luke said. "And she gave me that headpiece and all."

"That's so," John agreed. "All right. That's what we'll do. A day or two before Thanksgiving we'll have a turkey shoot."

But two days before Thanksgiving there was another snowstorm—a worse one than before. It started about nine o'clock, after John had left for Middleboro, and all day it came down thick and heavy, drifting against the fox pen and the shed, some places as high as Luke's waist.

At ten o'clock that night there was still no sign of John.

"Just as well," Mrs. Mitchell said. "He'd never get through these drifts, anyway, and might get stuck somewhere on the road. He's found a place to stay in town." She looked at Luke. "What's the matter?"

"The turkey. We were going to get the turkey tomorrow."

149

"Well, we couldn't help the snowstorm. And you wouldn't want your brother to catch sick . . . or worse . . . trying to get home for the sake of a turkey, would you?"

No, Luke thought, he wouldn't want that. But the thought of the turkey and the Princess and Thanksgiving got all mixed up in his head and he couldn't sleep that night. In the early, early morning, at the first light of dawn, he hopped out of the warm bed and crept downstairs to the hall closet.

There was Pa's gun, cleaned and oiled. Luke had done that himself, with John watching. He had shot the gun once or twice, with Pa, and killed a rabbit. He had never laid hands on it by himself.

Pa didn't exactly make a rule about it, and he wouldn't put the gun away somewhere. "On the average of once in a man's life," he used to say, "there'll come a time when he needs his gun in a hurry, and it's no good to him put away somewhere. The trick is to know when that one time comes."

This was not such a time, Luke knew, and he couldn't make himself reach up and take the gun. He must have stood there ten minutes, turning it over in his mind, when he heard a soft rustle behind him and turned to see his mother standing there.

"Let me give it to you," she said, "and then you

won't be burdened. With John away, you're the man here. I know you'll manage yourself right with the gun."

That was all she said, and it was all she had to say.

When he returned in the early evening, dragging his turkey behind him, John was standing on the back porch. He had gotten a ride on the town snowplow, and walked in from the main road.

"Didn't want to miss Thanksgiving dinner," he explained. "That's a fine bird!"—just as if he naturally expected Luke to go out without him and get the turkey.

"It's such a big one," his mother said, "what would you say to having the Princess come to us for Thanksgiving? Then she could take what was left back with her. Of course, it's for you to say, Luke. It's your turkey and your present."

"You could tell her it's like the first Thanksgiving," John offered. "The Indians were the guests at that."

Luke liked the idea. He didn't know how the Princess would cook the turkey anyway and, as Pa said, the Princess was a practical woman.

When he left the next morning, his mother was mixing up things in the kitchen and the smell of sage was all through the house. The storm was all over and the sun was bright, turning everything into a

151

starry white blanket. He had to plow through shoul-
der-high drifts at the shore, but wind had swept the
lake almost clear, and the ice rang under his heavy
snow boots. He looked back at White Banks, capped
now with snow, like a picture of the Swiss mountains,
and it was strange to see the forest white instead of
green. He thought how small he must look: one dark
speck in all this blinding white world.

It was a long walk across to Indian Shore, but not
as long as rowing, and Luke was surprised to find the
Princess out away from shore, squatting over a round
hole in the ice. There were two fish lying beside the
hole and she pulled another one out of the water
as he came up.

"Swish!" she said, pointing to the fish, and grinning. "Swish! Uh, Chasatonga?"

"I caught your turkey," he said, "and my mother's
cooking it. Will you eat? Thanksgiving dinner, I
mean. Today. Now."

"Huh," she grunted. "You wait."

Luke thought how easily she moved over the ice.
Most people took careful steps, one foot in front of
the other, afraid of slipping, but the Princess walked
straight and steadily, toeing in, till she disappeared
up the path to her house.

When she came back, he saw that there were

strips of wool wrapped around her legs and she was wearing high boot-like moccasins, maybe two pairs, and her blanket was over her head.

It was hard going back because there was more wind, and Luke would have been glad to stop and rest, but the Princess kept right on, head ducked low. And of course he couldn't stop if she didn't.

Dinner was ready when they got to the cottage. His mother had set the table with a fresh white cloth, and there were sprigs of holly-berry in the middle. It was special for Thanksgiving, he knew, and for his guest, but the Princess didn't take any notice. Too practical, he guessed.

They sat down and his mother looked at the Princess. "We say grace," she said, "before we eat, if you don't mind."

"To God," Luke added. "The Great Spirit. Thank-you, for the food."

"Ah-h-h," said the Princess, and she did a strange thing. She flung her head back and her arms straight up, and so she sat while his mother said the table grace.

Then she ate. How she ate! How they all ate! The turkey was crisp and brown and juicy, and there were potatoes and squash from the garden. The Princess ate everything with a spoon, except the turkey; that she ate with her fingers until she saw Luke using a fork, and then she tried that. His mother had opened a jar of watermelon pickle, and it was plain the Princess had never eaten that before. She made a face at first, but then she took more and still more, and Luke knew there would be a jar of watermelon pickle added to the turkey she would take home.

When dinner was finished the Princess lit her pipe, and Luke saw his mother gasp and cover her mouth, but she didn't say anything. And John lit his pipe too, and they sat in silence, smoking.

It was late afternoon when the Princess started home and the sun was slanting down on the horizon. It would be dark before she got across the lake.

"I could walk across with you," Luke offered, "or John."

The Princess only looked at him, but the look said as plain as day that she could walk across the lake, or anywhere else, with no help from anyone.

Before she stepped out on the ice she took a heavy leather pouch from the folds of her blanket and handed it to him. In it were the arrowheads, the needles—all the things from the burial ground.

"Why . . ." Luke was astonished. "These are yours. I gave them to you."

"I am an old woman," she said. "The Princess Wee-

154

tonawammet is an old woman. She will die. You take this strong medicine."

"Do you want me to bury them? Back on Minitik?"

"You keep. You. Chasatonga."

Then she walked off across the ice in the fading light, her blanket wrapped around her . . . the last of her tribe.

Luke watched as long as he could see her, and then started back up the path. He was worried about the relics; if he took them home John would see them and wonder, and his mother. But there was no other place . . .

He stopped suddenly. There was a place. There was his cave, his secret cave, under Council Rock. What better place to keep his . . . the Princess had said, his strong medicine.

He called in the kitchen door, so his mother wouldn't worry, and then went off up the path. It was harder to find the cave now, in the snow, but his arrow blazes were high enough to see.

He was looking for the brambles when he spotted something else through the trees: a quick flash of red . . . no more. But he knew. He knew!

"Tokala!"

He looked again. There, in a clump of pine trees, he was! Poised, paw in the air, ears tilted forward.

"Tokala!" he called breathlessly.

The fox turned then and came, stepping daintily on the snow, to his side. He nuzzled Luke's hand, and waved his brushy tail over his back.

"You do remember, after all this time." He could hardly believe it. "I don't have any bread or anything to give you."

Still Tokala followed him as far as the mouth of the cave. Then, off in the woods, there came the clear bark of a fox, and Tokala froze. He seemed to hesitate a minute—no more—and then was gone again, into the trees.

But he was alive, and he remembered! There would be lots of time to find him again: not to pen him up, or even take him home, but just to say hello from time to time.

Luke climbed through the brambles at the cave's entrance and laid the leather pouch close up against a wall, under a rock shelf. And then, because the cave was so dark and so cold, he left, satisfied that the Indian relics were safe and in "a place apart."

As he walked home the cold pinched his nostrils and his breath was a cloud before his face, and far behind him in the forest he heard the fox bark again —the only sound in all the quiet winter world.

It was only Thanksgiving! There was all the winter ahead, and spring, and then summer again . . . and all the years to come in the cottage by the lake, in the middle of the pine forest.

"*Low Bill, the Whaling Man,*" he sang, his voice echoing through the still night, "*A whaling man from Bedford town!*"